MOONLIGHT & MISCHIEF

MYSTERIES OF MOONLIGHT MANOR
BOOK 1

MOLLY FITZ

TRIXIE SILVERTALE

Moonlight and Mischief: Paranormal Cozy Mystery : a novel / by Molly Fitz and Trixie Silvertale — 1st ed.

[1. Paranormal Cozy Mystery — Fiction. 2. Cozy Mystery — Fiction. 3. Amateur Sleuths — Fiction. 4. Female Sleuth — Fiction. 5. Wit and Humor — Fiction.]

1

Today was the day. I knew it as soon as I saw the appointment pop up in my work calendar. My boss—who just so happened to also be my boyfriend—was finally going to propose. This was the fairytale ending I'd dreamed of as a homely little girl back in Iowa, and I'd sacrificed everything to put all those unpleasant memories behind me.

First, I'd swapped my thick glasses for contacts, then I fixed my overbite, and, finally, I made a habit of spending half my monthly income at the best salon in the city to keep my frizzy hair looking sleek and silky. No hint of the former farm maid remained, and that's exactly how I liked it.

Obviously my hunky hero liked it that way too, considering he was most assuredly on the verge of requesting my hand in marriage. He kept dropping little hints about big changes at work and casually referencing our living arrangement, both of which made me suspect. But when he set our appointment for today, I knew it for sure. And now I glided through the apartment with wings on my heels.

Honestly, I'd never imagined secretly dating my boss. When I took an entry-level job at the company, I was nothing more than a glorified social media influencer—which is code for coffee fetcher. Lucas Aconite, on the other hand, was a media god. His legendary company was the whole reason I'd moved to New York in the first place.

Everyone at the agency worshiped him, and I was no exception. I worked twelve-hour days and took any extra unpaid overtime that was thrown my way. Growing up on a pig farm had taught me two things: 1. The value of hard work; and 2. That I would do anything to escape a future on said farm.

When my posts on the socials started going viral, I at last caught his attention. Let me assure you, once someone caught the attention of Lucas, they'd do anything to keep it. I could still remember the way my heart stopped beating when he asked me to meet him at a posh club in Midtown after clocking out. And I swear, being there with him, it was like time stood still. The gaze from his smoldering hazel eyes could do that.

Initially, we kept our relationship secret, but once the accounts I managed got first national—and then international attention—no one could doubt that I'd earned my position at the top. Once my integrity was no longer in doubt, I wanted people to know that I was so much more than a lowly account manager to Lucas. Indeed, I had risen through the ranks and now stood on the cusp of leading a massively successful social media firm.

At first my guy resisted the sparks between us, but after a few work parties, and some carefully curated rumors—the Lucas-Sydney power couple was born. Everyone referred to us as Luc-ney. We became *the* #powercouple, and we took Manhattan by storm.

So, back to today's appointment, and why I know for a fact it will end with a champagne toast to our happily ever after.

You have to understand, Lucas and I just didn't make appointments with each other. I'd walk into his office anytime I needed to speak to him, and he'd walk into mine. When I saw his formal meeting request, I knew he absolutely had to have something special planned, and I couldn't keep the smile off my face.

I'd been dreaming of the possibilities all morning.

My favorite version involved him whisking me off to Alfonso's. It was impossible for mere mortals to get reservations there, but you didn't run the top internet marketing firm in Manhattan without getting your share of hookups. And Alfonso's would only be the beginning.

My day was off to a great start. My hair looked fantastic, and I couldn't get over the way the light made the ebony hues in my perfect blowout shimmer. Pinterest-perfect hair was worth every penny. The only rain cloud in my morning was a burned out lightbulb in the temple sconce in the bathroom. When the lighting was dim, I could see the ugly duckling, lurking just beneath the surface, leaking through.

I couldn't afford to have an episode of self-loathing right then. I had to be the "it" girl that had captured his heart, not the misfit from swine-ville. It was all nearing its fairytale end. Of course I'd be quick to take the Aconite name and pretend the old me had never even existed once upon a time.

I poked my head out of our bathroom. "Lukey?" I paused to listen, but he didn't answer. "Lukey, I need you to change a light bulb for me."

Usually, he'd respond immediately when I called

him. After all, it wasn't like him to leave for work in the mornings without saying goodbye. We meant more to each other than that. Now where had he gone?

I walked down the wide hallway of our modern, steel-and-glass penthouse apartment and peeked into the open-plan kitchen and living room. I'd come a long way from scrubbing the floors of the farmhouse kitchen and cooking tubs of food for hired hands.

But the perfectly designed and decorated living space was empty.

As I continued toward the spacious home office, I thought I heard him speaking in hushed tones inside. Something made me stop and listen outside the door. I bit my bottom lip to curb my excitement. Maybe he was setting up final details of his proposal day.

He sighed. "Look, babe. I know you're in a hurry, and I'm moving things along as fast as I can. I told you, I'm firing her today. This whole Sydney mess will be over by the end of the month. Relax. We've made it this long, so what's a couple more weeks?"

Sydney mess? Who was he going to fire? *Me*? That couldn't be right.

Wait, who was he talking to, and why was he calling her "babe?" My impulsive, demanding side kicked in before I could stop it. I placed my perfectly manicured, ring-less left hand on the door and shoved. The door slammed into the wall behind it.

"Lucas, honey, who are you talking to?" I asked in a eerie sing-song voice I hardly recognized as my own.

If guilt had a meme, it would be my boyfriend's face right now. "Uh, I gotta go." He unceremoniously ended the mysterious call and stared at me while his jaw hung slack.

"What's going on?" My fists clenched and landed on my hips. I plastered a pleasant smile onto my face. Though, it probably looked more like a snarl. I was desperate to hide the fire of hurt burning in my golden eyes, and the growing ache in my fractured heart. "Who was that?"

Lucas composed himself, dragged a hand through his soft brown hair, and got to his feet. "Hey, Syd. I heard you calling me. Did you need something?"

"Yeah. I need to know what the heck you're cookin' up." The tough girl act would only hold back the tears for so long, but I couldn't ignore what I'd heard. "And with who."

"Man, you always get so hick when you're mad." He inhaled sharply. "Look, Syd, we both know things have been—"

"Been what? What are you talking about? Things

are great. Fantastic, actually." The tears were pushing hard now. Had he heard the crack in my voice?

His exhale was labored and his shoulders rolled back. "Sydney, it's over. Your work has been slipping. The partners are complaining about my girlfriend getting preferential treatment, and yesterday, you lost us one of our biggest accounts."

"What? Which account? No one told me." My throat tightened, and I couldn't swallow.

Lucas dropped his gaze, shuffled some papers on his desk, and checked his phone. "Listen, we don't need to get into it. You'll get two weeks' severance pay plus your third-quarter bonus, and you have until the end of the month to get moved out of the apartment. Don't make this harder than it has to be."

And . . . cue the waterworks. "Me? I'm not making this anything. Everything was great. Perfect! I thought you were ready to take our relationship to the next level, and now—"

"That's the problem, Syd. You and I don't see this relationship through the same filter." Lucas shoved his phone into his pocket, walked toward the door, and brushed past me without so much as an "excuse me."

"Fiddlesticks."

He snorted.

But I continued. "Where in tarnation do you think you're going, Lucas Aconite? This isn't over. You can't fire me without cause, and you can't kick me out of our apartment." The faces of every playground bully that had ever called me four-eyes or pig girl swirled before me. How could he treat me like I was nothing?

The chiseled face that turned toward me was almost unrecognizable. There was no love in his cold eyes, and no kindness in his words. "It's my company, Sydney. I can fire and hire whomever I choose. And this isn't *our* apartment. It's my apartment. You may have wiggled your way in, but you have no legal right to stay. Find somewhere else to live or I put your stuff on the street in two weeks."

I wished I had a snappy comeback or a defensible position, but I didn't. My dry mouth silently opened and closed as he turned and walked out of my crumbling life without a backward glance. The slam of the door reverberated through my chest.

Part of me wanted to follow him and talk some sense into his thick skull, but deep down, I knew Lucas had the upper hand and would always get the last word. Within minutes, I'd already reached the end of my short list of options.

Leaning against the door, I let the tears fall. There

was no way I'd be walking back into that office to face the judgmental stares of my former coworkers. Hopefully, I could get my assistant—make that *former* assistant—to grab some stuff from my desk and drop it off at the end of the day.

Unemployed and about to be homeless. Two weeks to find a new place to live, in Manhattan, with no references and no job. Good luck to me.

Hold on. I shouldn't throw the baby out with the bathwater—an "it" girl like me had tons of friends. I grabbed my phone and started swiping through contacts.

"Hey, Kasey, it's your girl, Syd. I was thinking about your plush loft in SoHo and wondered if you could use a new roommate to finance that fab design upgrade you're always talking about?"

She claimed to have no idea who I was. Not the response I'd expected.

"Sydney. Sydney Coleman. We have hot yoga together, remember?"

Either she honestly didn't remember, or couldn't be bothered.

Fifteen phone calls later, a familiar theme had emerged. The friends I'd thought were mine had all moved on. When I turned my sights on the elusive

Lucas Aconite, I simultaneously turned my back on everyone and everything else.

I'd achieved my couple status at the expense of the rest of my previously important relationships. All my eggs had been in one basket—a basket named Lucas.

I sank to the floor. None of my so-called friends were interested in a charity case. And, yes, one of them even used that exact phrase to deny me.

Charity case. Me. I was mad as a wet hen. There was absolutely no way I could afford an apartment in Manhattan—alone.

Once I'd moved in with Lucas, he took care of everything. My salary basically paid the minimums on the credit cards I used to keep my fantasy life afloat. Of course, that meant I couldn't put first, last, and an outrageous security deposit on any of those maxed out credit cards either.

Maybe it was time to admit defeat. My stomach turned when I imagined tucking my tail between my legs and running back to Iowa. To the farm. To my parents.

I shuddered. No, I would do anything but that.

If I thought finding out my New York friends had abandoned me was depressing, I couldn't imagine the horror of moving back in with my parents.

Old Mom and Pop Coleman would be more than happy to welcome me back from the "big dangerous city." But they weren't the problem. The problem was everybody else.

When I graduated from high school and announced I'd be skipping the college track in favor of a more exciting life in the Big Apple, no one was impressed. I was so determined to make all those people who'd tortured me and called me names jealous; I fabricated several details of the dream job opportunities that awaited me.

By the time I'd landed at Lucas Aconite's company, it seemed I'd finally made good on all the lies. Looked like today was the day I'd eat crow pie. Or was it just crow? Who knew? I was always messing up those folksy phrases my dad bandied about.

The one thing I knew for certain though?

I'd rather die than go back to Iowa.

2

My little situation rapidly devolved. To the point that dying was now a viable option on the table. I grimaced. No, not really, but it sure felt like it. Hopeless didn't begin to describe where I'd wound up.

A scheduled post, meant to hint at my supposed engagement, had gone live before I remembered to cancel it. The image of me with my left hand over my face, and the caption, "Today's the day." now made me look like a complete idiot.

Truth was, the self-delusion had made me an idiot, and now it was all over social media for the public to consume. The truth of my current reality stung. Now I had to come up with a new plan.

My once shiny hair was now scraped into a messy

bun, and I'd exchanged my designer dress and hooker heels for yoga pants and an oversized T-shirt. I now epitomized *Messy hair. Don't care.*

It was hour four of my frenzied internet search for housing. My low-cal chia seed smoothie went down the drain twenty minutes ago. This particular pity party called for double-chocolate mint-chip ice cream alternated with handfuls of kettle-cooked potato chips.

The level of desperation had pushed the boundaries of my search all the way into New Jersey. A place I'd sworn never to visit, let alone live. New York City was supposed to be my oyster—my smashing success, and I'd promised myself to accept no substitutes.

However, getting fired in a world where everyone knew everything in the flick of an update had disastrous repercussions.

Word had made it up and down the street—or rather the web. The darling of the Aconite Agency was so "last news' cycle." No more viral videos. Subscribers vanishing faster than purses at a Prada annual sale. I wanted to blame Lucas, but how much of this had been my fault? How long had I been feeding a fantasy of my own making?

It was lonely at the bottom of the barrel. No followers. No likes. No shares.

The only way to survive was to get out. I lifted my chin, determined to be down but not out. Options would be found, and I would embrace them.

Time to expand the search radius farther up the East Coast. Anything with a ZIP code starting with a zero was better than shoveling manure at Mom and Pop's pig farm.

* * *

HOURS LATER, SEATED AT MY EX'S TABLE, A LOUD YAWN ESCAPED, and I rubbed my eyes vigorously. Maybe the next one would be—

"Hold on, I can afford that. Hallelujah. I can afford that." I scrolled through the listing that was finally in my price range and poured over the details, growing more and more thrilled with each syllable.

"Wait . . . This is in Massachusetts. I can't live in Massachusetts and work in New York City," I said to myself, seeing as I was currently my only friend.

My cell phone pinged with a new batch of Google alerts for my name appearing on the internet. All of them bad. Another ping made me cringe.

"On second thought, Massachusetts could be the fresh start I need."

As I dialed the phone number, I crossed my fingers and hoped someone would answer. Success. "Hi. I'm calling about the listing for the suite. Is that still available?"

The voice on the other end of the line confirmed.

"Oh, great." I had to set the phone down and tap speaker. My hands shook so badly I could drop my cell at any moment. "Can you tell me a little more about it?"

A thick Boston accent permeated the room. "Yeah. The place is wicked awesome. It's got a private entrance. Fresh paint. Furnished. Ready to go."

"That's great. And it's a one bedroom?"

"Yeah, that's right. One bedroom, one bathroom, and a walk-in closet." A scuffle started on the other side of the line, and I cringed as I listened to the fight in real time.

"Oh, wow," I murmured. The listing hadn't mentioned anything about a walk-in closet, but I loved the sound of that. "And is there a full kitchen, or is it a kitchenette?"

"Bobby, stop punching your sister. Patrice, defend yourself." There was a crash and a child screamed.

"Yeah, we got a full kitchen. You got privileges. You know?"

Hmmm. Kitchen *privileges*. The price was starting to make more sense. "So, there isn't a kitchen in the suite, is that right?"

"Cam, I swear, if I have to tell you chowderheads one more time—" Feet pounded across the floor in the background, followed by shouts. "Yeah, you come in and use the kitchen anytime you want. We're all family, you got it?"

Oh, I didn't want to get it. There was no way. I didn't want to touch this with a ten-foot pole, let alone with one of my finely manicured hands. Echoes of farm hands and lively arguments across a wooden-plank table loomed. "How many kids do you have?"

"Five for now. Bobby Senior says we ain't done 'til we can field a whole team. So I figure he can slip one through the five-hole, and we'll get that goalie added to the roster this year." The woman sucked in a long breath. "Eddie. Ray. Get off the counter!"

"That's nice." This couldn't be my only option. I wouldn't let it be my only option. I'd look harder and find something else I could make work. As the woman continued to regale me with the perks of this magnificent apartment over her garage, I absently scrolled through the additional listings. I didn't remember hanging up on her, but it would hardly matter.

My forehead hit the table, and I mouthed a silent prayer to the universe. *Please send me an actual option.* I raised my heavy head and feared it was time to admit defeat. A thumbnail caught my eye. A click later, my fingers clutched the edge of my chair. Too good to be true?

There was no way to be certain if my eyes—red and bleary as they were—had deceived me. If this cute house in Maine—

I was already dialing the realtor. "Hi, I'm calling about the house for sale in Misty Meadows."

Her tone was dull and lacked any genuine conviction. "Sure. What did you want to know?"

"Is that price correct? Is it for rent or for sale?" The pictures were amazing and if that sale price was real, I could buy this house outright with my severance package. *Please be real.*

"That's the price. Did you have any other questions?"

It didn't really seem like she wanted to sell the place. "Is there a catch?"

"No catch. The family just wants to sell the property. Did you want to come take a look at it?"

"I'm in New York. I don't have a car."

Her entire demeanor changed and her volume doubled. "Oh, you're a flatlander. You'll love it here. Misty Meadows is a gorgeous town, and the manor is in remarkable condition for a historical building. You should take the train up from Penn Station and spend the night. That will give you a chance to look at the property and explore the town. I promise, you'll love it here."

Now that was the sales pitch I had expected. "Sure, I'll figure out the train schedule and call you when I get into town. Is there a hotel?"

"I've got a friend up the road apiece with a bed-and-breakfast who owes me a favor. They stay pretty booked up, but I'm sure I can get you a night there, free of charge. Let me know when you get into town."

The call ended, and I blinked. Was this the answer to everything? An affordable home in Misty Meadows? I continued to scan through the photos. The architecture was stunning. Gothic, yet elegant. It was no Manhattan penthouse, but it was a far cry better than skulking back home.

I could already picture the feel of the vaulted ceilings, arched windows, and ornate details. Plus, the flying buttresses lent a touch of whimsy. I wasn't sure how I felt about the random leering gargoyles, but they added character of some sort. Buying it outright meant no rent and a lot more wiggle room for my future career. Whatever my next career became.

A flicker of my fight came back to life. New York City didn't know what it was losing. I had a brilliant skill set. If the other bed-and-breakfast place stayed booked most of the time, I could turn this breath-taking historic landmark into the bed-and-breakfast of the century. Maine was the fresh start I needed.

So then it was decided.

Misty Meadows, get ready for Sydney Coleman.

# 3

Now that I had the semblance of a plan, I was feeling less helpless nerd-girl and more avenging angel. My comeback would be glorious and epic and everything I imagined it to be.

Lucas always worked late, and after issuing his ultimatum that morning, I was reasonably certain that he'd grab dinner—and probably several drinks also—before returning to the penthouse.

Fine by me. I'd be ready when next I saw him, and he would be distraught that he'd foolishly let me slip through his fingers. Of course the real question was how much groveling I'd make him do before agreeing to take him back. And I suppose the even realer question was whether I actually believed he'd grovel at all. He'd been so very mean that morning.

I stormed into the master suite, grabbed one of his duffel bags, and loaded all of my toiletries into it—high-end makeup samples I'd received free as part of various paid partnerships, exclusive hair products, and some bougie face creams that weren't even commercially available yet.

The bag was heavy—weighted down with the spoils of lost opportunities. I carted my haul into the guest suite and cried as I unpacked.

"I'm keeping the duffel bag." Having said it aloud, through my cascade of tears, the room seemed to agree.

I made my way back to the gorgeous walk-in closet in the master to retrieve my precious designer wardrobe and move it into the guest room.

Nineteen trips later, I was forced to admit, my couture was awfully Manhattan-centric. This field trip to Maine would have to serve double duty. I could check out the property and get a feel for local fashion. Some of my pieces could be reworked, but my new life would most likely require a new wardrobe. Not that shopping was a bad thing, but it wasn't in the budget right now.

The train schedule seemed simple enough. I

studied the route: grab a train to Boston at Penn Station, change trains in Boston, and, from there, head to all points Maine.

Then I packed an overnight bag, which contained a very scaled-down version of my facial routine. After setting my alarm, I stared at the four walls and groaned.

The woman scorned part of me wanted to hack into my ex-boyfriend's email and solve the mystery of the other woman, but the tiny, wounded Midwestern girl cowering deep within my heart convinced me to take an Ambien and cut my losses. Forget it. *Forget him.*

* * *

When the gentle notes of the harp-tone alarm slowly ramped up, I opened my eyes and smiled. For a split second, yesterday's catastrophe had been forgotten, and I snuggled down into the luxurious bedding.

Don't worry, it all came crashing back in the blink of an eye.

"Fiddlesticks." That was something my sweet Gran always said, and uttering it out loud was a way I honored her memory. She'd lived to see me succeed, and as much as I missed her, I was happy she didn't have to witness my downfall.

My goal for the day was no tears. So far, so good. But I had to grit my teeth against the onslaught to keep it true. Maine or bust. I would turn myself into the ultimate comeback story.

Light makeup and a high pony would be the extent of my efforts this morning. High-waisted flare-leg jeans, a flouncy, boho-chic blouse, and a brown leather bomber jacket completed my look. I didn't own anything less than a three-inch heel, but a chunky-soled L.A.M.B. boot did the trick. As I reached for the handle on the guestroom door, a twinge of panic gripped my heart, and I blinked back the threatening waterworks. What if he was still here?

Nope. I didn't owe him an explanation for anything. I held my head high, marched down the hallway, and out the front door. If he was in the apartment, he wasn't any more interested in talking to me than I was in talking to him.

The door closed softly behind me. I pressed my fingers against the dark wood and forced myself to whisper, "Good riddance." Maybe if I said it enough times I could make myself believe it. I hurried off.

Penn Station was busier than a fox in a hen house.

I had grown so used to taking a private car to work every day, I'd forgotten how innocently my life in New York had started. I was jostled, bumped, and at one point possibly groped, but eventually I got my ticket and boarded the train to Boston.

Traffic out of the city on a weekday was light, and I was grateful for a seat all to myself.

After I changed trains in Boston, an elderly woman sat next to me and gave me the play-by-play while she knitted a scarf for her grandson. Crossing my fingers, I hoped she wouldn't turn her kindness on me. I knew that if she said one nice thing directly to me—I'd start crying my eyes out in two seconds flat. Luckily, she disembarked in southern New Hampshire and my tears stayed safely locked away.

I dozed off twice on the rest of the journey, but anticipation gave me a burst of energy when they announced my stop. If I could work out the details, Maine would be my new home.

There were only three people on the platform. An elderly gentleman, a delivery person in uniform, and a bottle-blonde in comfortable, two-inch heels.

The blonde waved maniacally. "Sydney. Over here, Sydney."

I quickly waved back, concerned she could dislo-cate her arm. That had to be Mia Jones. Realtor extraordinaire. Her current hyped-up state was nothing like her initial subdued phone presentation. Maybe she was having an off day when we spoke on the phone. Happened to the best of us, didn't it?

"Hi, Mia. Thank you so much for meeting me at the train."

"No problem at all. Let's jump in my SUV and get straight out to the property. I want you to have as much time as you need."

Her tone was beyond excited. It seemed like she yelled the entire greeting, but her face showed no sign of strain. Apparently, she was what I'd heard people refer to as a "loud talker." We could've used someone like her to call the farmhands in from the field.

However, her generous manners made me forget about the volume. She offered to take my bag, carefully placed it in the back of her vehicle, and opened my door before moving on to her own.

Gorgeous scenery rolled past my passenger-side window, and I stared in wonder. The new sights made Manhattan fade. My post-rejection pain lessened an undeniable degree or two.

Mia grinned as she gazed out the front windshield. "So, what do you think so far? Aren't these pine trees amazing? They don't call it Pine County for nothing."

With a work-smile firmly pasted on my face, I engaged in the necessary small talk and struggled to mask the hurt in my heart. "It's quite beautiful. Absolutely worth the trip. I hate to get straight down to brass tacks, but you know how us New Yorkers are." My attempted chuckle was met with an instant challenge.

"Aw, you can't possibly be a New Yorker. You're far too nice, and you have the voice of an angel."

Did she just call me a liar? My inner victim wanted to take offense. "I've been living there for the past six or seven years. It's all such a whirlwind, but worth it."

She nodded and chewed her bottom lip.

If I didn't know better, I'd say she doubted my story. Time to double down. "I work for the top internet marketing firm in Manhattan, but it feels good to get out of the city."

"Oh, you're not planning on living at the manor?" There she went with that lip chewing again.

"I'm taking a sabbatical. This project will definitely help me refocus my purpose." I didn't love lying to her, but I couldn't possibly bare my jilted soul to a woman I met five minutes ago.

"Well, Misty Meadows will take good care of you, honey."

Choosing to ignore the term of endearment that threatened to pop the top off my pain, I shifted the focus back to her. "Are you married?"

She took a deep breath, and a placid smile spread across her face. "Three years divorced. Best three years of my life. I gave that man everything. Then he wanted to live in Mississippi. Can you imagine? I'm an East Coast girl. There were other issues, let me assure you, but that was what I like to call the straw that broke the camel's back."

If memory served, that's what everyone called it, but I didn't come here to debate idioms or aphorisms. "I'm looking forward to seeing the manor. I have to be honest, though. The pricing definitely concerns me. The photos tell the story of a pristine Gothic mansion with incredible architectural details. The price makes it seem like a hoax. I hope you don't mind me saying?"

Her thumb thumped on the top of the steering wheel and the seconds ticked by. "It's been on the market for a long time. Not everyone wants to live in Maine, or live in such an interesting piece of history. The family kept lowering the price, and I kept renewing the listing. At some point, I suppose it became my white whale." She guffawed and ran a finger under each eye to swipe away imaginary tears. "In my heart, I always believed the right person would find it and something tells me today is that day."

I admired her reference to Herman Melville's epic tale. As a teen, books had literally saved my life. When the bullying and the name calling got to be too much, I'd disappear into a book, or three, and pretend my life was far away from the frizzy-haired nightmares in Iowa.

So, if by "right person" she meant someone desperate enough to ignore all the red flags and warning sirens, she'd be right. If this thing had a solid roof and running water, I'd take it. I knew what I could do with a diamond in the rough.

4

The red-tinged maple leaves peeked between swaths of green and hinted at the approaching autumn. Mia turned off the main road at the freshly painted "Moonlight Manor" sign, and the warm afternoon sun disappeared behind a thickening pine forest, while the long and winding drive approached the hidden manor with a sense of hesitation.

When we made the final turn, the mansion loomed into view and took my breath away.

"I had the same reaction the first time I saw it, honey." Mia parked near the base of the impressive grand entrance and scurried around to open my door.

I knew everything there was to know about internet marketing—followers, subscribers, likes, boosts, and going viral—but I knew next to nothing about architecture. Well, I knew what I liked, but I didn't know why or what to call it. Not to worry . . .

Boisterous, max-volumed Mia to the rescue. "As you can see, Moonlight Manor is clad in rusticated granite and the front elevation is composed of two distinct towers. The one on the right is cylindrical and adds a little bump-out to the first floor drawing room and second floor main suite. The top of that round tower is trimmed with what's called egg-and-dart molding and capped by a conical Tyrolean roof. Technically, that's more of a Scottish Baronial feature, but because the home was built during the Gothic Revival period, it's still classified as Gothic."

I hated to admit, I had no idea what she was talking about. However, it sounded awfully impressive. She skipped up the wide stone staircase leading to the ground floor of this three-story beast. Make that three stories plus a possible attic.

Mia stopped outside the arched wooden double doors and gestured for me to follow. For some reason, I couldn't move my feet. The place had me so awestruck I felt as though it put me in a trance. My attention was fixed on the beautiful wraparound balconies on the second level and the entire ground floor. Maybe on the ground floor it would be called a porch? Anyway, intricate wrought-iron railings curved around both, and there seemed to be chimneys everywhere. Such delicate stonework . . . And is that a bronze dragon bursting out of the main gable?

Oh, look at me. I remembered what that was called and everything.

"Don't be distracted by the grounds, Sydney. I know a great landscaper. I can have this thing whipped into shape for you in no time."

I hadn't noticed. But now that she'd mentioned it, my eyes roamed over the grounds and there was a distinctly wild and abandoned vibe. To be honest, it didn't bother me in the least. I knew plenty about cutting grass and planting flowers. Before she offered up any additional suggestions, I hurried up the broad granite steps and waited while she retrieved an ornate skeleton key from the realtor's key box looped through one of the massive front door handles.

"You could always have this re-keyed. Of course, there's a certain charm to keeping things original, but as the new owner, you can do as you please."

New owner? Could I be the new owner? I liked the sound of it. Something entirely my own. No one could kick me out, or— Before I had a chance to sink too deeply into that daydream, Mia steered me through the home and described all that we surveyed.

"All the fireplaces are French marble, and the pointed-arch windows in the living room and library are the original leaded glass." She waved a hand to the right. "This webbed tracery in the archway that separates the hallway from the drawing room needs a little repair, but it's completely original. Oh, I forgot to mention before we came in, the second tower on the left, the hexagonal one, adds a bit of a bay window feel to the library, on the ground floor, and the study above."

What would I do with a study? Who cares? It was mine, and I could do with it as I pleased. I had to say, I was loving the towers.

Mia guided me into the library, and I finally noticed all the furniture. "Is the entire manor furnished? I saw the sheets on everything, but it didn't click right away."

"Everything is here." She nodded and gestured to the shelves. "Even the books."

My heart leapt in my chest. *Books.* I wanted to stop and comb through the shelves, but my tour guide moved on.

Mia walked toward the tall, narrow windows. "The oak leaves in the stained glass are an ode to the past. I believe there is still one large oak on the property, but sadly, most of them were felled for construction and furniture. Of course, some of the furniture"—she stopped and flipped back a sheet covering the desk in the library's corner—"like this piece is something called acid-treated sugi wood. It was imported from Japan. Apparently, the acid turns the wood black as coal. Quite fascinating, don't you think?"

I nodded, but I had no words. We circled through the kitchen, formal dining room, ballroom, and she pointed out the fresco ceiling above the massive chandelier in the foyer.

There was so much going on, I had totally missed that when we walked in.

"The imperial staircase will take you up to the second level, where you'll find the bedrooms, the sitting room, and the study. The domed skylight above the double-height stairs offers beautiful natural lighting. Don't you think?"

On the second floor, I followed her mutely through one stunning bedroom after another. Thick Persian carpets covered most of the hardwood floors, and gilded edges of hidden picture frames poked out from behind more sheets.

The gorgeous, beamed ceiling in the sitting room separated more detailed frescoes. Now, I'd lost count of the number of fireplaces. "How large is this mansion?"

"Let's see . . . The listing says eight-thousand square feet. Not including any of the outbuildings. Which is good. Because most of the outbuildings are in what I like to call disrepair. Luckily, the stone construction of the main house and its slate roof have stood the test of time."

"How much time? When was this built?" I stopped to admire a beautiful pane of stained glass depicting some mythical Celtic scene, and as my fingers traced the rich colors, Mia's voice cut through my fog.

"They originally started construction in 1862. Although, I've been told it took more than eight years to complete. So technically, it wasn't finished until sometime in 1870." Mia led the way to a tightly twisted, circular oak staircase leading to the some-what smaller third level.

"Up here you have servants' quarters, a sewing room, and a studio which I believe was used for painting. The northern exposure gives a lovely, even light."

A narrow door at the end of the hallway seemed to call to me. I glided toward it, unable to resist. As I gripped the robin's egg blue glass knob, Mia called out. "Oh, that's just a tiny stairway up to the attic. Hardly worth the trip."

As loud as her voice was, it couldn't cut through the compulsion. I twisted the handle and climbed the steep stairs into the pointed pinnacles. This room, this whole space, was different. This was the home of secrets, and the dusty, slightly decomposing scent of history. Of all the places in this gorgeous and unspeakably refined manor, this was the room that convinced me. "I'll take it."

A strange half gasp, half squeak echoed up from the base of the ladder-like steps. "Oh, Sydney. You're going to love it. Did you want a forty-five-day escrow or do you need sixty?"

I walked to the top of the stairs and light poured in through one of the bluish circular windows, punctuating the tiny dormers along the front of the house. The warmth crept across my skin, into my bones, and welcomed me. "Actually, I was sort of hoping for a ten-day escrow."

Mia literally stumbled backward and clutched the handle of the door to steady herself. "Oh, my goodness."

The next part was somewhat mumbled, for her, and I wasn't sure if I was meant to respond. So, I returned to my exploration of the magical attic. All the while, I caught bits and pieces of Mia's soliloquy.

"Well, I can handle that part. If it's all cash, we can waive the inspection. Paul Martin knows someone at the county records office . . . I can fast track those documents, and I think my sister-in-law is still a notary to boot."

A strange silence descended, and I watched dust motes dance in the beams of sunlight that painted the light-blue walls. There was an old spinning wheel, several trunks, some sort of cloth mannequin, and a poofy red velvet cushion. The cushion was well worn in the middle, and surrounded by tattered, cloth cat toys strewn about the floor. They looked handmade.

How sad. A family and their beloved pet. Made you wonder...

"Sydney, honey, if we're gonna do this in ten days, we've got to get back to town. I'll drop you off on Main Street and head into my office to get started on this paperwork. If you can give me a couple of hours to make some phone calls, gather my thoughts, and draw up the contracts, we might be able to make this happen. Can I ask why you're in such a rush?"

The girl from Iowa wanted to spill all my beans, but the Manhattanite "always take selfies from your best angles because social media posts are forever" side of me refused to let down my guard. "My sabbat-ical won't last forever, and I really want to get going on my project. This place is perfect."

"And just to confirm, you did say it was a cash offer, right?"

Pressing a hand on either wall as I teetered down the sloped staircase, I nodded. "Yes. All cash. And, sorry if I didn't answer. You can absolutely drop me on Main Street. I should be able to entertain myself for a couple of hours. It will give me a chance to get to know the town better. Right?"

"Of course. Did you want to see anything else before we leave?" Her tone seemed generous, but her body language screamed *get back in the car.*

"Not today. Thank you so much for showing me this place. I absolutely love it."

5

The drive back to town seemed to take half the time. The injured part of my heart still ached with the pain of Lucas's rejection, but the idea of starting a brand new life filled me with an energy I hadn't felt for almost three years. The thrum of excitement was intoxicating.

Mia pulled to the curb and stopped. "I'll text you when I've got everything together, and you can let me know where to pick you up."

"Thank you. Is there any place that is an absolute *don't miss*?"

She chuckled and pressed a hand to her chest. "You haven't lived until you've been to Heaven Can Bake. Main Street is filled with cute little shops that cater to tourists, but that bakery is what I like to call a local favorite."

"Perfect, I'll check it out." I stepped out of the vehicle and closed the car door. I was never one to miss a place with five-star reviews.

Mia drove off, and I meandered down the quaint street. Traffic was light, and there were only a few pedestrians on the sidewalk. The complete opposite of Manhattan. And if I was completely honest with myself, I didn't miss the hustle and bustle. I passed a drugstore, a pet supply shop, and a locally owned hardware outlet called Martin & Son. But, so far, I'd only been window shopping. When I caught my first whiff of the recommended bakery, I decided to buy something.

Heaven Can Bake knew its market. The striped awnings were inviting, and the large windows gave you a clear view of the delicious pastries inside.

I pushed open the door and inhaled deeply. This place smelled like everything I'd been denying myself for years.

Not by choice, mind you. There was an unspoken rule at the Aconite Agency. If you let yourself go, you were gone. But this . . . This smelled like freedom from the old and embracing the new.

Lucas never came right out and told anyone to

lose weight or buy better clothing, but everyone knew. If you put on a few pounds, you lost a few accounts. If you showed up to work with chipped polish on a week-old manicure, you didn't get invited to the presentation for the next big client. And the agency was an equal opportunity discriminator too. The guys at the shop were held to the same standards. If they let their man-scaping go, they would find themselves getting coffee rather than new accounts. Without exception, people got the message, and they left—generally before anyone had to make anything official. In the six years I'd worked for Lucas, I'd only seen him fire three people. Unfortunately, one of those people was me.

"You look like a woman who could use a caramel-apple cupcake with cinnamon buttercream frosting." The curvy, pleasant woman behind the pastry case smiled warmly.

Unconsciously, my hand brushed against my hips and I worried about the calories. I had eaten my scant allotment of carbs in secret for so long; I wasn't sure if I dared to allow myself a public exception to the rule. I'd promised myself the pity party ice cream was a one-time thing. "Oh, that's all right. I was just looking. I'll have a coffee. No sugar. Thanks."

The woman shook her freckled face, framed by

messy red curls, and grabbed a black stoneware plate. "Have a seat by that table at the front window. Nobody window shops at my bakery." Her laughter was generous and forgiving.

I smiled self-consciously and slipped onto a chair that gave me a lovely view of Main Street and a spot in the warm sun. What an encouraging difference acceptance made.

Moments later, the woman approached, juggling a scrumptious-looking cupcake on a plate, a fork and napkin, and two coffees. She placed everything on the table and pulled out the chair opposite me. "I'm Frannie Clark. Owner of Heaven Can Bake." She pushed the cupcake toward me and winked. "I don't know what you're running from, but this will help. I promise I won't tell any of your friends back in New York."

Her oddly accurate perception unnerved me. "How do you—?"

She brushed away my concern with a flick of her wrist. "Oh, don't worry. It's nothing spooky. When you run a place like this, you learn to read people. Folks are real honest when it comes to their pastries. And the New York thing was a lucky guess. Your haircut looks about five minutes old, and that wardrobe screams Fifth Avenue. I've been there, and I'm happy to say I'm never going back."

She had my attention. "What do you mean?"

"I'm only a couple of years older than you, and we seem like we may have followed similar paths. I had to get out of my Podunk hometown and prove to everyone that I was more than a freckle-faced carrot-top. So I spent my early twenties going to the right schools and getting the right jobs and making obscene amounts of money. But inside, I was empty. All the glitz and glamour of the big city and the fat paychecks couldn't fill my soul. I knew I couldn't give up and go home a failure, but I also knew I had more in me. Does that make any sense?"

I was leaning forward eagerly and nodding my head with every syllable. "I know exactly what you mean. That's essentially my story, except it was buck-tooth and four-eyes."

She tilted her head to the side and nodded. "I'm a Kansas girl. You?"

My heart warmed for the first time since Lucas had dumped me. "Iowa."

She laughed out loud and slapped her healthy thigh. "Oh, sister. I don't have to tell you. I know you may not be ready to talk about it. Like I said, I've been there. But I gotta ask, what are you running from and where are you running to?"

For some reason I wanted to tell Frannie everything. The contacts app on my phone was littered with fake friends, and I'd never connected with any of them the way I had with this kind woman in under ten minutes. "My name is Sydney Coleman, and I'm a recovering target of bullying." I sighed with relief.

She grinned. "Welcome to Misty Meadows, Sydney. I like you already."

Frannie sipped her coffee, and I told her my tale of woe. "So I kept widening the search area until I found this amazing place for sale in Misty Meadows. I took the train up this morning, and I just finished looking at the property. I'm going to buy it. I'm going to be a homeowner."

Her mug of java clinked against mine. "Congratulations. Let me be the first to welcome you to town. Which place are you getting?" She took another slow sip of her coffee and waited for my reply.

"It's a little ways out of town. It's called Moonlight Manor. Have you heard of it?"

She grabbed the napkin and pressed it to her lips to prevent an unpleasant coffee-related scene. "Honey, everyone's heard of it."

And there went the red flags and sirens again.

"Please tell me it's not too good to be true. I have no other options. I want a fresh start, and that place would make such an amazing bed-and-breakfast. Doesn't the other place stay booked?"

"Most of the time," she said.

"Then I think I can do it."

Frannie leaned back and squared her shoulders. "You know what? I support your decision. When I walked away from my six-figure New York City income to open a bakery in a tiny town no one had heard of in Maine, I got nothing but negativity. I didn't even tell my parents. All the dire warnings from my so-called friends were enough. But look at me now. I love what I do. I have plenty of customers, make a comfortable living, and my heart is full."

My eyes got a little misty at the corners, and I blinked back my tears. Longing flooded me. "That's what I want. I want to do something, not just get up every day and measure myself against some unrealistic standard of beauty and success. I want—I want what you have. Not a bakery, but the full heart bit." A hopeful smile lifted the corners of my mouth.

She arched an eyebrow. "If you're going to start a bed-and-breakfast, I hope you know how to cook."

A rapid montage of me in the kitchen back in Iowa flickered through my mind. I could make huge vats of chili. I'd brewed gallons of coffee. And there was the occasional use of an oven, with mom's supervision, to roast a pork loin for a special occasion. But the majority of my recent experience with high-end food involved calling people who delivered it. My shoulders fell, and I gazed down at the table. "Yeah, not so much."

Frannie crossed her arms over her ample bosom and smiled. "Well, I've got all sorts of experience. Every bed-and-breakfast needs a signature breakfast item. I'd be happy to help you out."

My eyes widened and my jaw hung slack. This woman, whom I only met today, had offered me more than any of my fair-weather friends. "Seriously? You would help me?"

Her brown eyes sparkled with mischief. "On one condition."

And there it was. Everybody wanted something. Not that I was in much of a position to argue, but I'd hear her offering to see if it was worth the trouble. "What's the condition?"

She reached toward the square black plate on the table and pushed the luscious cupcake to me. "You take one bite. One enormous, messy bite and if that isn't the most delicious cupcake you've ever eaten—"

I stared at the cupcake as though it was a giant

subway rat. Flashes of the body-shaming gossip at the Aconite Agency surfaced, and I struggled to push that twisted life behind me. "If I take one bite, you'll help me plan a menu for the bed-and-breakfast?"

Frannie nodded. "I'll do you one better. I'll provide all the breakfasts on commission. If you don't have guests or if they don't like the food, you don't have to pay me." She pointed at the glorious confection. "One bite of the world's best cupcake and you essentially get free meals for your bed-and-breakfast. How can you lose?"

My mouth was already watering. "Deal." I hesitantly picked up the cupcake, peeled the paper, and turned the frosted behemoth back and forth as I attempted to plan an attack strategy.

"Just open your mouth and shove it in. I promise you won't regret it, Sydney."

I took a deep breath, steeled my nerves, and opened wide.

In an instant I was Meg and Charles Wallace Murry, and this cupcake was my portal to another dimension in *A Wrinkle in Time*. My eyes rolled back in my head and my body swayed from side to side with sheer ecstasy. Light fluffy cake, gooey caramel center, and this amazing cinnamon frosting.

"They always say that silence is the best reaction.

But I'd like to hear what you really think." Frannie leaned her elbows on the table in anticipation.

I swallowed the amazing explosion of flavors, wiped the frosting from the corners of my mouth, and sighed in satisfaction. "That is literally the best thing I've ever eaten. You are a cupcake goddess."

She grinned and reached her hand across the table. "Looks like we have a deal, Sydney Coleman."

I wiped the cinnamon buttercream frosting from my hand and eagerly gripped hers. "Oh, we have a deal, and you have a best friend for life, Frannie Clark."

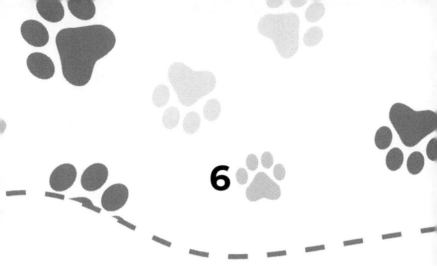

6

The papers were signed. I'd done it.

I owned my own home outright, and I intended to carry the confidence forward. Nobody discounted my bed-and-breakfast idea, and even Mia had been encouraging based on the steady business at her friend's place.

On the train back to New York City, I felt like a queen carried forward on the shoulders of a throng of admirers. The success bolstered my courage and made me feel as though I'd made the right choice to leave my heartbreak and the big city behind. Also, if Lucas thought I was going to leave quietly, he was wrong.

In my absence, he'd returned to the apartment—

assuming he'd defeated me. I could use that to my advantage.

He opened and closed cabinets in the kitchen, probably looking for something I'd been responsible for putting away.

I marched into the room and crossed my arms. "Hey, I wanted to let you know I found a place and I'll definitely be moving out at the end of the month."

He peeked out from behind a cabinet door, and the pleasure of victory that spread across his face sickened me. "I'm glad you see things my way, Syd. It's good we're not going to make a mess of things."

Exactly. I wasn't about to make a mess. Instead, I would make a statement. No one was ever going to bully me again. "Oh, I couldn't agree more. The movers and the truck will be charged to the company account. Consider it part of my relocation package."

The muscles in his jaw clenched and unclenched several times. He was surely practicing the careful breathing technique that allowed him to remain calm and collected in even the most intense negotiations. "That's not what we discussed."

I placed my hands on the countertop and leaned forward. "Correct. We're discussing it now. You only gave me two weeks. If you want things to remain pleasant, you'll agree to my terms." My heart raced, and I feared I might lose my nerve at any moment. "And I think you want things to remain pleasant, don't you?"

The crooked vein in his left temple, that I used to find adorable, bulged to life. "Fine. If that's what it takes to finish this . . . Fine."

Unbelievably, things were working in my favor. I had to stay strong through to the end. Now I needed to make the final push. "You should know, I'm deleting the @AconiteSydney social accounts. I'm shutting them down on all platforms. I made the name, and I don't plan on leaving my hard work in someone else's hands."

His large hands balled into fists at his side, and he took three steadying breaths. "You're in an at-will employment/work-for-hire contract. That doesn't include taking work products when you leave."

I gave myself a quick pep talk and forged ahead. "This was also supposedly a monogamous relation-ship—*with my boss*. I'm shutting down the accounts, and you're lucky I'm not filing a wrongful termina-tion lawsuit. It would be easy, and I would absolutely walk away with a fat settlement. I'm as eager to put this disaster behind me as you are. Don't push me, Lucas. You'll regret it."

His entire demeanor shifted in the blink of an eye.

He was the master of knowing when to walk away. Lucas bowed his head patronizingly. Then he sauntered out of the kitchen and into his office.

I slowly exhaled the breath I hadn't realized I'd been holding and shook like a deer who'd just escaped a pack of wolves. I'd done it—on my terms. I'd bought my own new home, and I had made it clear I wasn't going to slink off into the shadows as though I wasn't worth my salt.

They say that breaking up was hard to do. I think I understood that at a whole new level.

7

t was moving day, and Lucas had made himself
scarce. I looked at the paltry stack of boxes, and
it was hard to believe my life in the Big Apple
had been so small. A few things were all I owned.
Had my existence been this empty the whole time?

There were a handful of pieces of furniture that
I'd chosen to take. Sure, Moonlight Manor was fully
furnished, and my modern pieces would look
completely out of place in that vintage setting, but I
paid for them with my own money and I refused to
leave anything for Lucas and his new girl-toy to
throw out.

As I dropped my set of keys on the polished zebra-
wood table in the hallway for the last time, I felt that
chapter of my life end. Grabbing my full-length

leather trench, I followed the last box down the stairs. Surreal didn't quantify the half of it.

I took the liberty of booking a company car to drive me to Maine, not because I had any issues with the train. It was simple. I wanted to push one more pin into my imaginary voodoo doll of Lucas. The image of Lucas getting the hefty bill tickled my fancy in a way nothing else could.

The long car slid into traffic, and I closed my eyes. Sure, it was corny, but I didn't want to sit in the car and watch the city disappear behind me. Maybe I was finished with New York today, but I wasn't willing to say it was finished—forever. Staring sadly out a car window, watching the memories slip past, wasn't how I wanted to leave. This would be a triumphant exit with my head held high. I had accomplished what I came to accomplish, and I was moving on to bigger, better things.

At least that was my story, and I planned to stick to it.

Frannie and I had been in touch over the passing days, and she'd agreed to stop by the manor to discuss all the menu options while I unpacked. Escrow officially closed this morning and Mia would meet me to handoff my key.

The past ten days had flown by, but I'd spent the

interim wisely. Using all the expertise from my years at the agency, I developed my brand, built my website, and set up listings on all the top travel booking sites. As soon as escrow closed this morning, I went live.

Bookings started almost immediately. My property was positioned perfectly. There were going to be reservations stacking out and I could honestly see turning a profit in my first month.

Things with Lucas ended about as badly as they could have, but I'd used my time and training at the Aconite Agency wisely. Moonlight Manor was going to be the most desirable bed-and-breakfast on the eastern seaboard.

The road rolled out in front of us like a red carpet, and my stomach settled. I had a plan. I had a great team, and after years of simply going through the motions at the agency, I was finally excited about what I was working on.

I stretched my back and laid my head against the seat. The next thing I knew, the driver was softly calling my name.

I sat up and blinked at the manor beside us. "Already here? Sorry, I must've dozed the time away."

He'd driven me a number of times over my years at the agency, and if he'd heard any of the current gossip, he was kind enough to pretend he hadn't. I unloaded from the vehicle and handed him a hefty tip. "Thanks, Mac. You're the best."

He took the money and gripped my hand with sincerity. "You've always been a real class act, Ms. Coleman. Right from the start."

The unexpected compliment brought a stinging moisture to my eyes and forced me to blink rapidly to hold back the tears. "Thanks for saying so. Have a good trip back to the city, Mac."

He nodded, hopped in the car, and offered a friendly wave as he circled around the fountain and exited the property. Part of me secretly hoped he would gossip mercilessly about my fabulous new venture. With any luck, curious Lucas would be one of my first followers on social media. The thought made me beam at my new home.

Frannie pulled up in her bright pink Suzuki Samurai, jumped out, and ran toward me. "Hey. I can't believe it happened. Congrats." She threw her arms around my shoulders and hugged me like the sister I never had. I'd grown up with two brothers, and anytime they came at me, it was for the sole purpose of wrestling or taking my food.

"Thank you. I'm so excited. I couldn't sleep last

night." Swiping a finger under each eye, I smiled brightly.

Frannie moved slightly and rubbed her hand warmly on my back. "Understandable. It's not even my deal, and I couldn't sleep."

The crunch of gravel under tires on the drive caused both of us to turn. Mia parked and walked briskly toward us. "I thought this day would never come." Her bleached-blonde hair was hair-sprayed into a snug French-roll.

I'd almost forgotten how absolutely booming her voice could be.

Mia rushed up the steps, removed the realtor's key box from the handle, and passed me my magnificent skeleton key. "This is one-of-a-kind, Sydney. I can't even begin to imagine where you could have a copy made. Guard it with your life."

I accepted the key, and I felt a strange tingle spread across my palm and flow up my right arm. The key itself seemed to repeat her sentiment. *Guard it with your life.* Weird.

Frannie nudged me. "Are you going to do the honors?"

"Right. My key. My house. I am the mistress of this domain. Let's do this." The key easily slipped into the lock, and I twisted it dramatically with more tingling shooting through my arm. Then I opened the door and crossed the threshold with an odd sense of anticipation and apprehension. However, as soon as Frannie and Mia rushed in, the nervousness vanished.

The duo walked through the house, pulling the sheets from the furniture and squealing in delight of each new discovery. I followed, surprised by the luxuriousness of every item they uncovered.

Mia headed upstairs and called down over the thick ornate balustrade. "My sister-in-law, Cheryl, has always wanted to see this house. She said she'd clean it for free if you let her poke around."

"Fine by me. I'm taking any and all offers for free labor."

Frannie laughed. "You'll have the whole town working here before long."

I scoffed. "Surely they've all seen it."

"Don't be so sure."

The friendly banter continued as we moved through the mysterious series of rooms.

Mia was the first to depart. "I made a list of some things that need repair. I'll stop by the hardware store and ask Paul to send his son out. Between them, they can get you an estimate."

"Oh, thank you." I hugged my arms around myself and smiled.

"Hey, it looks like you don't have a car." She jerked her thumb toward the driveway. "What do you plan to do about that? You're too far from town to walk."

The thought hadn't occurred to me. I hadn't driven since high school, back in Iowa. A car wasn't something one needed in New York City. "No idea. Do either of you know anyone who has an extra car I could borrow for a few weeks? I'll have to buy something eventually, but I can't really swing another big expense until some of my reservations start paying out."

Mia shrugged. "I found you free housecleaning, and I'm sure I can convince the Martins to cut you a screaming deal on these little repairs. That's it for me, honey. But I'll let you know if I hear about anything." She turned and took one last look at the beautiful imperial staircase, which split at the first landing and offered a flight of stairs to the left and right, leading to the second floor. "I'm going to miss giving tours of this place, Sydney. I hope you're happy here."

My smile widened. "Oh, I already am."

As soon as Mia departed, Frannie gripped my arm and whispered. "I didn't want to say anything while she was here, but I brought you a little box of food basics to get things started. Being a former city girl, I was pretty sure you wouldn't have a car, and I didn't want you to starve."

I tilted my head and smiled. "Thank you. And if I didn't say it before, thank you for being so nice to me and helping me. It's kind of a new thing."

"Which part is the new part?"

"The being nice to me part."

Frannie winked. "Don't sell yourself short, Sydney. I'll go grab the food—and the cupcakes. Mia can eat her weight in buttercream. That's another reason I wanted to wait until she left." She ran out to her car, opened the back, and balanced an enormous box precariously on one thigh as she closed the tailgate.

"Do you need help?"

"Nah. I toss fifty-pound bags of flour around all day long. I can manage a few staples and some baked goods."

Regardless, I held the door open for her when she returned. As she walked toward the kitchen at the rear of the house, she offered yet another helpful suggestion. "You know, the car thing got me thinking. I have this friend, Craig. He's a lobster fisherman and an avid cyclist. He hardly ever uses his car, and he cycles everywhere. I'm sure I could convince him to lend it to you for a week or two while you get everything sorted out here."

Wow. This woman might be my fairy god-sister. "Again, thank you. I'd ask you to spend the night and share a bottle of wine, but I know you have to open the bakery at the crack of dawn."

She dropped the box unceremoniously on the counter and swiped the back of her hand across her forehead. "Don't I know it? Speaking of which, I need to get back into town. Call me if anything comes up. Otherwise I'll see you when I see you."

I walked down the grand granite steps and into the drive, waving as Frannie's pastry-box-pink vehicle circled the ornate fountain and disappeared around the first turn. When I looked back at my mansion, something was different. The detailed bronze dragon bursting from the gable seemed to quiver with life. And the gargoyles perched atop the cornices surrounding each of the towers had eyes only for me.

Gulp. Maybe I should have asked Frannie to stay. Nonsense. My imagination was only running away with me, and I was a big girl who would absolutely enjoy spending her first night alone in her own private manor.

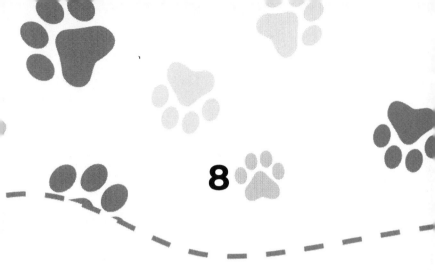

8

The sun slipped away far too quickly, and I found myself scurrying from room to room, turning on the retro-fitted electrical fixtures. I had to repeat the orientation speech to recall how Mia said they worked. "The mother-of-pearl button on top is 'on' and the black button on the bottom is 'off.' " Apparently, the home had originally been plumbed for gas, but sometime before the last direct descendent passed away, they'd upgraded everything for the newfangled invention of electricity.

Thank goodness. With only one person—*me!*—looking after the place, I couldn't imagine spending hours every afternoon, lighting gas lamps and preparing for the oncoming darkness.

My small stack of boxes peered at me from the polished parquet floor in the foyer. They could wait until tomorrow. Instead, I picked up my two suitcases, my large Gucci satchel, and my laptop bag, and headed up to the smallest bedroom on the second level.

Even though it was my house, I could charge a far higher price for rentals of the spacious main suite and large bedrooms. And the so-called small bedroom I had chosen was still twice the size of the guest room I'd most previously occupied in the New York penthouse.

After I climbed the wide staircase, I dropped the bags onto the Persian rug inside my new room with a sigh. I grabbed a washcloth and towel from one of my bags and headed into the bathroom to erase the day's strain.

The small round buttons in the wall plate clicked back and forth, but nothing happened. For a moment, I felt like *The Boy Who Harnessed the Wind* and had a dream of electricity. Shoot. I hoped this was one of the items on Mia's fix-it list.

Well, there were at least six other bathrooms—that I knew of—so I headed over to the master suite on the other side of the manor, to take the opportunity to soak in that glorious tub.

Hooray. The light switch worked, and there was actual hot water. Granted, I had to let it run for a few minutes to shift the color from rusty-brown to something in the vicinity of clear, but it was fantastically hot.

Before I could fully relax, I was forced to run from the cozy blue room to the cavernous burgundy room a few more times to fetch the necessary toiletries, but eventually I sank into the mound of bubbles and smiled. The heat eased the stress of the last weeks from my bones.

I raised my hand as I imagined every proud owner of this place had before me. Frothy bubbles dribbled down my forearm. Then I cleared my throat and spoke in my best imitation of a mistress of the manor. "I, Sydney Coleman, am the proud owner of Moonlight Manor."

"I should say so. The announcement is well past due, fair lady."

The breath in my chest seemed to freeze like ice. My imagination was running away with me once more. Dramatics never paid, as Gran always said.

The lights flickered, and I was torn between the urge to leap out of the bathtub and sprint to somewhere else, and the urge to protect my modesty. What if somebody was really out there? Some neighbor I didn't know about or some other person.

"Hello?" I called. "Who's there?"

Silence was the only response.

"Frannie?"

Still nothing.

Huh. So I'd imagined it. *Obviously*, I'd imagined the disembodied voice. People had all sorts of stories about spooky old houses, and I was here in this creaky, drafty mansion, all alone. The stress of the day was playing tricks on my mind. That had to be it.

Dipping my washcloth in the still-hot water, I tried to put the occurrence out of my mind. The large Egyptian cotton washcloth soaked up the luxurious bubbles, and I squeezed the warm liquid over my tight shoulders. "Let it go, Syd. It's nothing a good night's sleep can't fix."

"Alas, if it merely took the sweet release of dreams, I assure you the problem would've solved itself decades ago."

This time, there was no debate. Somebody spoke to me . . . from an empty house. I rocketed out of the tub, grabbed a towel, and fled back to my bedroom.

Slamming the door to the blue room behind me, I leaned against it with my breath coming in rapid gasps as I pushed on the light. Who could be out there? Who let themselves into my home? It wasn't Frannie or Mia. The voice hadn't belonged to either of them.

What the—? Well, if stress or exhaustion were to blame, somehow my eyes had now joined my ears in the charade, and I scanned the room, stopping short. Now I could only gape.

In the middle of my glorious, hand-carved mahogany canopy bed sat a large black cat. And if it was possible to say that a cat could look simultaneously royal and impudent, that was what I saw. How did it get there?

His lithe body—and somehow I was certain the feline was male—stretched, and he pushed himself into a lordly sitting position. "Good evening, madam. I am Sir Bogart. His Royal Felineness, Bogart the First, the Only, the Eternal." He licked the back of his paw and smoothed his whiskers patiently.

I shook my head and backed into the door behind me. "It's official. I've lost my mind. First, I lost the boyfriend, then the job—it only makes sense that the mind would be the next thing to go."

The black cat peered at me, untroubled by my words.

I pressed my towel-clad body against the blue-flocked wall and inched toward my suitcase in front of the fireplace.

"Ah, humans. How I've missed their feeble minds and endless justifications. You can hear me. You can see me, and yet you doubt the very senses which guide your daily life." The arrogant feline leapt from the bed in a single majestic bound. He slunk across the carpet, his black fur catching the light as his shoulder blades and hip bones moved in opposing rhythms.

I merely observed as the talking—*talking!*—black cat moved.

He came to a stop in front of me and paused expectantly as though waiting for me to speak. "Have you anything to say?"

"Don't hurt me," I began, trying to decide if maybe Frannie had slipped something into my baked goods. "Listen, I have no idea what is happening right now, and I'm sure this is a dream, but what do you want? Just tell me what you want."

He dropped lazily onto one haunch and his velvet rope tail curled slowly around him like the elegant cloak of a long forgotten king. "My list of wants is long and refined. History has taught me that the two-legged species are unable to meet most of my high-brow demands. However, you appear to be a quick study. I require entertainment. I've not had a decent distraction in ages. We can discuss the details at length. But first, I insist you solve the mystery of my murdered mistress."

Great. Not only was I seeing cats that didn't exist. Now the bossy little man was crying murder. How was I supposed to help a cat with solving a murder?

A thought then struck me.

"Oh, my gosh. Is this some kind of sorority hazing ritual? Are Mia and Frannie in on this? I get it. Play a prank on the new kid. Pretend you're all leaving her alone on her first night in town and then spook her with a holographic ghost cat." I tightened the towel around my torso and took a deep breath. "Joke's over, guys. You really had me going for a minute there."

Silence. No friends shouting "gotcha" from the ground floor.

"Guys? Seriously, it's not funny anymore. You got me. You can come out now." I winced when no one answered. "Come out," I repeated, but my voice trailed away as my panic ebbed.

The regal black cat tilted his head in concern. "Perhaps you possess less wit than I assumed. I shall break it into smaller pieces for you. I am trapped on this infernal plane of ignorance. Lo, for these many years, I've sought escape from this punishment. At last, I have deduced that solving my mistress's murder is my only recourse. The truth will be my only release from this tribulation. As the new owner of Moonlight Manor, you, and you alone, are privy to my secret world. In addition to this rare gift of my inimitable presence, you are also privileged to behold me in all my glory. I am a magnificent specimen in death, as I once was in life."

Some part of my exhausted brain decided to simply roll with it. "And so modest."

Sir Bogart's mouth dropped open and the tip of his lavish pink tongue lolled out of his gaping maw. "You jest. You are the first of your kind in more years than I care to count who has had the temerity to joke in the face of my fierce magnificence."

I shrugged. "Crazy, right? I mean, I bought the place furnished. Maybe I hadn't expected it to include some ghost-cat-beast, but what choice do I have?"

Sir Bogart did not speak but observed me through slitted cat eyes.

I continued. "Nevertheless, chalk it up to spending the last few years in New York. Once you've shared a subway car with a rat the size of your child-hood dog, not a lot of things really scare you. So, Sir Bogart. You and I are roommates?" Glancing around,

I leaned in. "And I'm not sleeping or dreaming. Is that correct?"

Sir Bogart didn't answer at first. Finally, he said, "Surely, that is another attempt at your weak humor. You are not sleeping or dreaming, Miss Coleman. Additionally, I am the Lord of this Manor, and I simply deign to allow your cohabitation. However, your presence here is solely by my will. Do not cross me."

I couldn't explain exactly where the courage came from, but something that he said, or maybe it was the way that he said it, reminded me of Lucas and his at-will-employment nonsense. Well, I was sick and tired of letting people bully me and push me around to get what they wanted out of me.

Holding my towel tightly with one hand, I stepped toward the spectral beast. "Listen. If you've been trapped in this house for decades, you're not the one calling the shots. You want me to help you solve some mysterious murder? Then you better start treating me with the respect I deserve. I'm the owner of this house. I'm the mistress of all I survey. And if you expect me to give a hoot about the wants and needs of a spoiled ghost cat, then you better *recognize*."

I got wrapped up in my role, and when I lifted my

hand to snap my fingers for emphasis, my large, wet bath towel hit the floor, and my cheeks caught fire. The falling towel hindered the impact of my proclamation. But still.

If it were possible for a cat to laugh, then this one cackled himself into a fit. It sounded like an odd combination of a terminal hairball and bones rattling in a long forgotten dungeon.

My face blushed six shades of red. I grabbed my towel, a handful of clothing, and raced into the bathroom. "No lights."

I'd rushed into the bathroom requiring a skilled handyman. Never mind. I could get dressed in the dark. I'd done it enough times in the past—up before dawn to slop the hogs and all that nonsense. No time to slip into a sad walk down memory lane. I needed to clothe myself and finish my fight with the feline apparition in my bedroom.

Struggling to get my wet arms through the sleeves of my oversized sweater, I grumbled loudly. Water still trickled down my face from my wet hair when I stormed out of the bathroom, intending to give the surly cat a piece of my mind.

Yet the bedroom was empty. Nothing on the bed. Nothing on the floor.

"Sir Bogart? Your Royal Felineness?" I whispered, unsure how much I wanted this pussycat to reappear.

Wow. Maybe my tantrum speech banished him. The physical exhaustion of the day, paired with the emotional stress of whatever had just happened, was biting into my bones. However, the imposing, curtained bed did not look inviting.

Grabbing a couple of dry towels and an over-stuffed throw pillow, I retreated to my couch in the foyer. And that would be my actual couch from my apartment in New York. Again, it didn't go with the décor, but at least it felt safe and un-haunted.

I curled up on the buttery cream-colored leather and covered myself with an assortment of laundry. The cat could figure out his own sleeping arrangement.

For hours, my eyes darted from one dark corner to the next. Every shadow of a leaf and whisper of a breeze sent a chill down my spine. Then I drifted into a world of broken sleep and mysterious messages...

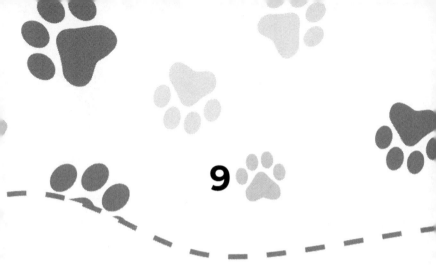

9

n my dream, someone pounded on the lid of my casket and I searched desperately through the satin-lined interior to find a release lever. My throat dried, and my stomach churned.

No way out. Had I been buried alive? I scratched at the bottom side of the casket, drawing my fingernails over the same place again and again. How had this happened?

When my eyes popped open in terror, it took me a moment to register the knocking was on the front door of the apparently haunted mansion I'd been so quick to purchase.

Rubbing the sleep from my eyes, I wrapped a robe around my shoulders and stumbled to the massive front doors. Haunted or not, there was no going back on the transaction, so I just had to find a way to spin it in a positive light for my future guests. I had no other options, and Sir Bogart, if he was real, could take a flying feline leap for all I cared.

The pounding echoed again.

Right. First things first, I needed to answer my door. Grasping the handle, I gave a hard tug. It creaked open with a long groan.

I blinked against the early morning sun, finally shading my eyes from the invading light. "Hi. Are you from the hardware store?"

The suntanned man on my porch smiled pleasantly and mirth danced in his blue eyes as he ran his fingers through his dark-brown hair. "I'm Craig. The *lobstah* guy Frannie mentioned."

As my eyes adjusted, they drank in the lovely vision on my porch. He had just the right amount of scruff on his square jaw, and his vibe was pleasant and inviting. My thoughts froze as I realized where I was mentally headed. Nope. I'd officially sworn off men. This lobster guy—and to be clear, he said *lobstah* with no "r" at the end—was a lovely distraction, but not for me.

I extended my hand, and he shook it pleasantly. "Did you say Craig? Nice to meet you. I'm Sydney."

"Sorry to wake you, but I gotta get to the boat. So

I'll leave the car in your driveway." He handed me the keys.

My brain finally caught up to what was happening. "Oh, you're *that* Craig. Thank you so much. I have a ton of errands to run. It's really kind of you to loan me your car."

"Not a problem. I'll grab my wheels and get outta your hair. Any friend of Frannie's is a friend of mine. You like *lobstah*?"

Who didn't like lobster? "I love it."

"Perfect. Maybe you and Frannie can figure out how to fit it in the menu for your fancy B n' B, eh?" He grinned and almost winked before he hurried away.

"Sure. That sounds wonderful. Thanks again." I waved and drank in the sight as he jogged toward the dark-blue SUV parked in my driveway. I'd sworn off *dating* men, not looking at them. He removed his bike from the rack on the back of the vehicle and waved once more as he rose in the stirrups and pedaled away. For the briefest moment, I had the smallest twinge of envy. He seemed as comfortable on a cycle as he was on his own two feet, and I observed his retreating figure until it disappeared from view.

Wow. Frannie was turning out to be a goldmine.

Helping me with the menu, finding me a temporary car . . . I'd have to think of some way to repay her.

"Do you have a moment to discuss possible options for entertainment, madam?"

Gasp. My heart rate spiked through the roof.

As I spun around with the hope that my ears had deceived me, it disappointed me to discover they had not. "Sir Bogart?"

"It is I. I have not met a human with your penchant for negotiation in some time. However, I have considered your terms, and I find them acceptable. I will attempt to meet you on an equal footing, and our parlay shall involve the give and take between equals."

This was happening. There were no more tired eyes or optical illusions hidden in the darkness. There was a ghost in my foyer. The ghost of a cat, and he was talking to me. When in Rome . . .

I squared my shoulders and glared at the small creature. "Good. I'm glad we agree on something. Now, I'm going to pretend all of this is normal and walk into my kitchen and make some coffee." As an afterthought, I glanced over my shoulder and added, "Please don't possess me."

His rattling cackle echoed from the high ceiling. "There is no need for such drastic measures, as long as we maintain an open dialogue. Although, I must insist that we move forward in solving my mistress's long dormant murder."

His ethereal form trailed after me.

Once we reached the kitchen, I swiped the coffee from the counter and then turned to him. "Look, Sir Bogart, I'm not trying to be difficult, but I'm not a cop or a private investigator. I'm a marketing expert, and one who recently got fired at that. I don't know the first thing about solving murders—fresh or otherwise." Or ghosts. What did I know about ghosts? Ghostly posts were good on social media at certain times of the year. That's what I knew.

"Fear not, my fragile human. I brought help."

Without warning, two human-shaped ghosts popped into existence in the middle of my kitchen.

Of course I screamed and dropped the bag of coffee grounds. The dark brown granules skittered across the floor. "What is going on?"

"I told you she wouldn't like it, Bogey. I told you." The one speaking looked like a former member of the kitchen staff. Her gray-blonde curls were tucked under some type of white bonnet, and her apron bore the stains of grease, blood, and a dusting of flour.

"Sir Bogart," I demanded. "What is happening? Who are these people—um, ghosts?"

The refined feline leapt onto the counter and gestured with an elegant coal-black paw. "This kind woman is Velma. She was my mistress's cook and kept me well stocked with chicken livers in life. A wonderful woman and you would be hard-pressed to find a cook in the state who could match her rack of lamb." He nodded with admiration in Velma's general direction and continued the introductions. "This fine gentleman is Norman, my mistress's butler and confidant. Norman knows all the pertinent secrets and will be of great assistance in our investigation."

The majestic cat dropped onto his backside and flicked a claw toward me. "Norman, Velma, please make the acquaintance of the new owner of our manor, Sydney Coleman."

Velma offered a silent curtsy, and Norman made a deep bow. "A pleasure to meet you, your ladyship," they intoned in unison.

Regardless of the fear coursing through my veins, I could get used to being called *your ladyship*. "Pleased to meet both of you. You'll have to excuse my fright. I'm not used to conversing with spirits. It's going to take some getting used to."

Velma bobbed two additional curtsies. "Of course, miss. Of course. Would you like me to make you a cuppa tea?"

"Oh, this is coffee. I don't really drink tea. Nothing wrong with it, but I'm absolutely a coffee person." I wasn't sure why I was using such an apologetic tone, but then I didn't know the latest on ghost etiquette.

"Leave it with me, miss." The ghost of yesteryear's cook scooped the actual bag of coffee from the pale-pin encaustic tile floor and stared at the machine in front of me with consternation. "Beggin' your pardon, miss. If you'd show me how to work this 'ere contraption, I'd be likely to improve myself and get your morning coffee started early on the 'morrow."

So, this was happening. I was teaching a ghost how to use a coffee maker, and she meant to make my morning "cuppas." I wasn't sure this day could get any stranger.

While I went through the motions of preparing coffee—filling the water reservoir, measuring the grounds, and pushing the buttons on the *contraption*, Norman marched out and began unpacking my boxes. I ran out of the kitchen, and left Velma to marvel at modernity, while I attempted to stop Norman in his tracks—or lack of tracks, as the case may be.

I gestured at him. "You don't have to do that. I'll take care of it later."

"Nonsense, madam. I see that you've taken the blue room, and I shall endeavor to arrange your personal effects to the maximum efficiency. Should I find any items that do not have a home in that space, I should consult you at once. Fear not, I have a sixth sense about these things."

I wasn't even comfortable arguing with the ghost of a cat, and now I'd have to bargain with a butler and corral a cook. This was supposed to be the start of my new life. But it seemed as though I hadn't so much bought myself a house, as I'd opened Pandora's paranormal box. Oh, and let's not forget, in the midst of moving in, and finding my way around a new town, and bargaining with spirits, I'd also be welcoming guests to this haunted mess.

Velma called from the kitchen. "I believe your coffee is ready, miss. The machine is hissing like an angry cat, and I should know. Anyhow, can I make you some breakfast?"

"No, thank you. I'll have one of the cupcakes Frannie brought."

As I returned to the kitchen, Velma floated around the massive butcher-block island and fretted over my last response. "Beg your pardon, but I don't see any small cakes in the larder."

I smiled at her innocence. Pointing to the pink

cardboard box, I explained. "The items from the bakery are inside there."

She looked at the rosy square and poked it with one finger. "It's made of paper. How odd."

Flipping back the lid, I showed her the delectable contents. "These caramel-apple cupcakes with cinnamon buttercream are unbelievably delicious. Do you want to try one?"

A sadness drifted across her face, and the glow surrounding her semi-corporeal body lessened. "The saddest part of this existence, miss. A cook can't taste nothin'. If you'd do me the kindness of describing it to me, I will try to remember the tastes from before . . . That part still works."

Despite the underlying tingle of fear that still gripped my gut, my heart hurt for her. Her admission made her seem something more real than a simple apparition. She had been a person with real desires and goals. . . and a *life*.

I carried my coffee and a cupcake to the small oak table in the corner and took a large bite from the confection. I described each sensation to the best of my abilities: taste, mouthfeel, and the way the mélange of flavors complemented each other . . .

Velma drifted above a chair, interlaced her callused fingers under her round chin, and smiled dreamily. "It sounds divine, milady. You have a skill with words."

"Thanks. You must've brought your former mistress much comfort with your kindness."

She smiled. "True. Norman and I figure we musta been our mistress's favorites. There ain't no other explanation for being trapped here between the worlds for so long. The three of us, we spent hours and hours, years actually, attempting to discover our purpose. Weren't till you arrived did any of us feel a flicker of hope. Perhaps you can truly solve this murder and help our mistress." Velma's eyes filled with tears and she dabbed at the salty drops with the corner of her apron. "I should leave you, miss. I apologize for acting so familiar. Isn't proper."

"No, no, it's fine," I began, not wanting her to feel out of place. After all, she'd lived here, before and after her death, longer than I had. It was her home for as long as she needed.

But she was already gone. I finished my coffee in silence and felt a sudden need to tell someone about the events that had transpired—both last night and this morning.

A quick trip into town, thanks to Craig, seemed in order. Frannie would know what to do . . . after she picked her jaw up from the floor.

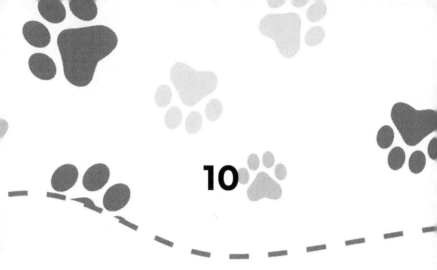

10

I took one last look around as I prepared to head into town. My phone was more than fifty percent charged, I had my one-of-a-kind skeleton key, and—

CRASH.

A stone hurtled through the stained-glass panel on the left side of my arched front doors and skipped off the floor like a stone on a still pond. I screamed and jumped backward as brilliantly colored shards of glass sprayed across the wooden floor.

Dropping my purse, I charged through the front door and shouted at the form retreating into the dense woodland on the side of the drive. Who could have thrown a rock into my house? My new home . . . my new business.

I flapped my arms wildly. "Hey. Where do you think you're going? Hey. Get back here."

The figure disappeared into the thick green ferns carpeting the forest floor beneath the elegant pines without a glance back.

I gritted my teeth. I had no idea what the heck was going on, but New York girls didn't scare that easy. I dialed 9-1-1 and reported the crime. The voice on the other end of the line assured me that the sheriff would respond immediately.

Well, it looked like I wouldn't be headed into town just yet. When I walked back into the house to see if any of my otherworldly associates had heard or seen anything useful. Yet not a ghost could be found. So that was how it was going to be. They would pop in when it suited them, but leave me high and dry the rest of the time. Great. More fair-weather friends. Then again, I probably shouldn't expect too much camaraderie from beings who were literally haunting me.

Hopping on my phone, I checked the latest reservations. I had my first guests arriving in three days. Mia's sister-in-law would be out to clean tomorrow, and Frannie would absolutely be able to put something together by the weekend. We'd call the first booking a soft opening, and I'd see if I could get the guests to post some fun photos with #Moonlight-Manor. The best way to stack out my bookings was going to be to throw all-in with a big social media push. The harder it was for people to get a reservation, the more they would want one.

Tires on the gravel grabbed my attention. I ran out onto the stone steps in time to see the sheriff exiting the black-and-white.

She smiled in a serious sort of way. "Good morning. Are you Ms. Coleman?"

"Yes. And you must be the sheriff." I walked toward the tall, athletic woman with her short brunette hair and extended my hand.

She shook it firmly. "Sheriff Haley Allen. I hear you had a little trouble this morning. Not the kind of welcoming committee we like to send around here. Did you happen to see the perpetrator?"

"I didn't get a good look. He—or maybe it was a she—ran into the woods in that direction."

"So, no clear look at the face?" She tapped her pen on her pad as she waited for me to answer.

"No. Sorry. Let me see if I can remember what they were wearing." I closed my eyes and tried to picture the shape as it melded into the forest. "The coat was long, and a little shabby. A dingy yellow, I think. Oh, and there were boots. Rubber boots, but black. Now, what are they called?"

The sheriff stopped writing and replied. "Galoshes?"

"Yes. And they might've been wearing a gray stocking hat. You know, a loose knit one." I shrugged, and couldn't remember anything else.

Sheriff Allen finished taking down the description, folded her notepad, and returned it and the pen to the front pocket of her coat. "I'll have a talk with a few of the neighbors and get this report filed for insurance purposes. Although, you're going to need someone who specializes if you plan on restoring that stained glass."

For the first time since the incident, I turned and surveyed the damage. The hole was just bigger than my fist, but the images of oak leaves in the stained glass were intricate and detailed. Not something I could simply purchase at a local store. "Gosh, I've got guests coming in a few days. Do you have any suggestions who to use?"

Sheriff Allen tilted her head, and her eyes widened in awe. "Guests? So this isn't a residence. You're running a business here?"

I wasn't interested in landing on the wrong side of the law on my first proper day in town. "Yes. It's all permitted and licensed. The realtor, Mia, helped me get everything taken care of. I'm running a bed-and-breakfast, and we filled out all the paperwork to pay the proper lodging taxes. Totally aboveboard. I promise."

Sheriff Allen waved away my worries with a smooth gesture. "Oh, I'm not one of *those* sheriffs. Misty Meadows is a great little town, and most of the folks around here are the type that would leave an extra penny in a dish before they'd take one. I'm sure you've taken care of everything you need to. Thing is, I'm more surprised that you were able to get guests into the house. You know— Well, I grew up hearing the stories."

My throat tightened, and I pushed the part of me that wanted to hear the old rumors back into a metaphorical box. "No ghost stories here. A fresh start. You know?" Images of my ghostly triumvirate flashed through my mind.

"Ayuh. You know how impressionable kids can be." She smiled brightly and gestured to her cruiser. "I'll drive around and chat up the neighbors. Maybe someone saw something. You can always count on the residents of a small town to notice an outsider."

"Thanks, Sheriff. Oh, hey, did you happen to have a suggestion for repairing this?"

She tapped her right temple and nodded. "Right. I guess I got sidetracked. You want to talk to Augusta Adams. She runs a little school here that keeps the old crafts alive—stained glass, brown ash basketry, all that sort of stuff. She's a great old gal and if she can't fix it herself, I'm sure she'll have a student with the right skills. Have a good day, Ms. Coleman. I'll let you know if I run across this vandal."

"Thanks, Sheriff. And it was nice to meet you."

She nodded, hopped into her vehicle, and pulled away. I returned to the house to see if I could locate a broom and dustpan. When I opened the door, Velma was hard at work cleaning up the mess.

"Oh, thanks."

"It's my duty, miss." She swept up the last of the glass, polished a light scratch on the floor with the edge of her apron, and floated toward the kitchen.

As she emptied the dustpan, I swallowed hard and broached a sensitive subject. "Um, Velma, I don't mean to sound ungrateful, but you're going to have to be more careful."

"Careful? Oh, I didn't break the window, miss."

"No. I know. There was some vandal that ran into the woods. What I mean is, once the guests start arriving, you can't be sweeping in the middle of the foyer anytime you please. I don't want rumors of ghosts scaring our visitors."

The generous, round cook turned, and her eyes flickered with vengeful flame. "Oh, you can't have guests, miss."

My spine chilled, and as I opened my mouth to protest. Norman appeared beside her. "Oh no, no, no. Under no circumstances are we in a position to entertain company, madam."

Sir Bogart, having also recently appeared, remained quiet, but the rapid, irritated flick of his tail confirmed he was in agreement with his cohorts.

"Look, I told Sir Bogart last night, and I'm telling all of you now, I'm the new owner. What I say goes."

The three ghosts exchanged an unreadable glance, but something in the flicker of their energy did not bode well for me. They all vanished with an audible pop and left me with a sickly unsettled feeling in my stomach.

The only thing I could do was keep busy and hope they wouldn't make good on their thinly veiled threats. I collected my laptop from the bag in my upstairs room and took a seat on my bed. Time to set up an appointment for a quote for stained glass repair.

Let's see if I could find this Augusta Adams person online.

A search brought up nothing, and I frowned. That wasn't possible. Everyone, at least every business, had an online presence of some kind in this day and age.

Closing my laptop, I hurried downstairs, ripped a flap off one of the cardboard boxes, and taped it over the hole in the window. The patch wasn't as pretty as the original, but at least it would keep insects out.

Vandals and stubborn ghosts could not stand in my way. I would drive into town and find this Augusta Adams myself. As soon as the thought popped into my mind, warm memories of my gran washed over me. One of her favorite sayings was, "if you want something done right, do it yourself." Well, here I go Granny. Your little Syd-bunny is doing it herself.

I breathed a sigh of relief when I climbed into Craig's vehicle and saw that it had an automatic transmission. Pop had tried to teach me shifting on the farm truck, but I always found excuses to get back to my books. Manual transmissions hadn't been worth my time since. Until that very moment, the thought hadn't occurred to me, but if Craig had left me a stick shift, I might have been just as screwed as I would've been with no vehicle at all.

First stop: Heaven Can Bake.

* * *

Frannie looked up when the gentle bell chimed at the opening of her front door. "Sydney. How was your first night?"

I raised my eyebrows, widened my eyes to saucers, and nodded toward a lonely table in the corner.

She smirked and covered her mouth with one hand and gestured me over to the private table. As soon as she finished ringing up the one other customer at the counter, she filled two mugs with coffee and joined me. "Your timing is perfect. This is the pre-lunch lull. I have at least twenty minutes, so talk fast and don't leave out any details." She wrapped both her hands around her mug and leaned forward eagerly.

"First of all, you have to promise me that what I'm about to tell you goes no further. I can't afford for a word of this to get out."

Frannie instantly lifted a fist and extended her pinky toward me. "I won't tell a soul. Pinky promise."

I hooked my pinky through hers, and we shook three times.

After two steadying sips of the bakery's luscious coffee, I spilled all of it. Not the coffee, just my news. The ghost cat, the towel drop, and the spirit servants.

She leaned back, rubbed her hand slowly around her mug, and grinned. "Craig put you up to this, didn't he? He's got quite a reputation as a prankster in this town. I should've known when I sent him out there to drop off old Blue Bell, he'd talk you into yanking my chain somehow."

The color drained from my face, and I leaned toward her. "No. I'm not kidding. Honestly, last night when I heard the disembodied voice and jumped out of the tub, I thought you guys were playing a prank on me. Frannie, I promise, I'm not making this up." I leaned closer and lowered my voice to barely a whisper. "My new home is legit haunted. Three ghosts. No lie."

Worry flashed through her brown eyes, and she twisted a red curl around her left finger. "You promise? People tell me I'm awful gullible."

"Hey, this is a mid-west sister promise. Maybe someone is playing a prank on me, but I'm telling you exactly what happened. And then this morning some nutter threw a rock through my window."

Her expression instantly shifted to concern. "A human person? Are you all right?"

"Totally a human person. And I'm fine. But the beautiful stained glass panel of leaves has a giant hole in it. It's the one on the left side of the door. Well, it was on the left when I was inside. So that'd be the right side from the outside?"

Frannie laughed, reached across the table, and patted my hand. "It's okay. It's the one with the hole in it. That should be pretty obvious."

We chuckled, and it felt good to share my burden with someone who genuinely seemed to care.

"I don't have any suggestions about your 'G' problem." Frannie made air quotes around the G, shrugged and winked. "However, Augusta Adams will be able to fix up that window lickety-split."

"That's what Sheriff Allen said. But I couldn't find any information on Augusta online."

Frannie nodded. "Augusta is unbelievably old-school. Do not mention worldwide webs or internets or hashtags to that woman. Her sole purpose in life is preserving the old apprenticeships and mentor-taught crafts. And she can absolutely fix that window. I'll draw you a quick map."

And with that, Frannie gulped down the last of her coffee, grabbed a napkin and pen, and drew me a semblance of a map. "Here you go, Sydney. Good luck. And, maybe don't mention the bed-and-break-fast either."

"Why? Does she hate tourists too?"

"It's not that. It's more about preserving the old way of life. I'm sure if you were opening an inn, where people had to write you letters with a quill pen to get a reservation, she'd be all for it. If you say anything about destination travel or online bookings, she'll lose it."

Pressing a hand to my stomach, I laughed. "Geez, navigating small-town life is a lot harder than I imagined. I really appreciate your help."

Frannie waved away my gratitude. "Don't mention it. By the way, what did you think of Craig?"

I blushed. "I'm sure Craig is considered a hot property around here. But I've sworn off men. I'm not saying it's forever, but absolutely for right now."

She smirked. "If you say so."

As I headed for the door, she waved and called out, "Tell Augusta I sent you. That might buy you some sympathy."

I smiled and waved.

Next stop: Adams School of Colonial Arts.

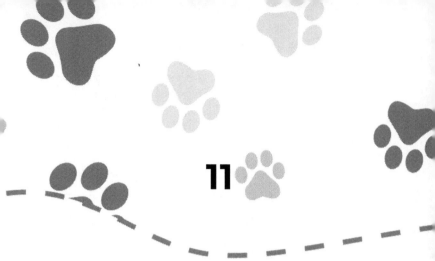

11

Frannie's map was easier to follow than it seemed. She'd drawn the location of a special forked tree that caught my attention and helped me find the almost hidden turn to the school.

As I approached the campus of the Adams School of Colonial Arts, I sighed. "Impressive. Looks like she converted a private estate. But I can't believe she doesn't have a website for this. She could make a killing charging for tours."

I angled into a parking spot and glanced to either side. Two other cars. I couldn't shake the vision of what I would be able to accomplish with a diamond in the rough like this. However, Frannie's warning echoed in my head and I promised myself I'd make no mention of online anything.

The large single door towered several feet above my head and led into a space warmly lit with indirect light. Lovely creations adorned the walls and small placards indicated which pieces were historic, and which had been created by modern artisans who'd learned the old techniques at the school. The skill of Augusta and her students did not fail to impress.

"If you're here for basket weaving, you're late." A full-figured woman brushed pale-blonde curls back from her lined forehead.

"Oh, I'm not a student. Frannie Clark sent me."

"Well, why didn't you say so? How is that old so-and-so?" She rubbed at some dried paint on her strong, weathered hand.

"She's fine. I'm looking for Augusta Adams."

"And what do you plan to do when you find her?"

Something told me I had, indeed, found my target, so I chose my next words carefully. "I recently purchased a historic manor outside of town, and one of the original stained glass windows needs repair. I want to keep everything original, but I can't have a hole in one of my front windows."

The pleased expression on her face gave me hope.

"I see. And which historic home do you think you've purchased?" Her brown eyes held a challenge.

"It's called Moonlight Manor. Have you heard of it?"

I'd started to expect the shocked and concerned expressions when I mentioned the name of my property. So, hers came as no surprise, but an extra layer of something lurked just beneath the surface. "Which window was broken?" She squeezed her eyes to slits and waited.

Sounded like she was more familiar with the property than most. "It's one of the panels beside the front entrance. On the right hand—"

Her face pinched with worry. "The oak leaves? How big is the hole?"

Wow. Had she been there recently, or was she a walking Wikipedia of all the antique stained glass in Maine? "It's about the size of my fist. Do you think you can repair it?"

She looked at me with a thin mask of tolerance. "Of course. I don't run a theoretical think tank. This is a school for artisans. We don't prattle on about pie-in-the-sky theoreticals. We get things done. It'll cost ya."

And that last bit was the precise phrase I'd hoped I wouldn't hear. "I understand. And I truly value the skills you're teaching here. It's just that I'm a little short on cash right now, and I'm trying to negotiate trades and favors. To be honest, it'll be months before the insurance money comes through. I don't have much to offer."

"Insurance? Did the break happen recently?" The creases in her forehead deepened.

"As a matter of fact, some vandal threw a rock through the window just this morning. I didn't catch sight of them, at least not their face. I only saw a mustard-colored coat disappear into the forest."

The expression on Augusta's face shifted from interest to something near rage. "Did this mustard coat have a head of messy gray hair?"

I paused to review the sighting. "It might've. I thought it was a stocking hat, but—"

Augusta pounded one fist into the opposite palm. "That gosh darn Gladys Williams. Don't you worry about money for a second. I'll be up there to fix that window this afternoon, and I'll take the payment out of Gladys's hide."

"Are you sure? How do you know it was her?"

"Trust me. You'll get to meet her face-to-face soon enough. I'm sure you've heard the stories about the manor being haunted, but if you ask me, that nosey parker Gladys is the reason they ain't been able to sell that place for fifty years."

Fifty years. No one mentioned that little tidbit. "I can't tell you how much I appreciate this, Augusta. I've got a box of Frannie's best caramel-apple cupcakes, if that means anything."

For the first time in our brief acquaintance, the no-nonsense woman smiled. "You should've started with that. I'd move heaven and earth for one of those cupcakes." She continued to grin, and sighed with pleasure. "Should be able to slip away in about an hour. I'll bring my supplies and get that window removed. I've got an excellent apprentice right now and we'll get to work on it right away."

I knew I couldn't use the arrival of my guests as any type of pressure to move the process along faster. "Do you have a piece of glass I can put in the frame while you're working on the repair?"

"Oh, pshaw. You don't need to put glass in there. I'll just board her up and have that stained glass piece back to you in about a week or so."

Shoot. Also not what I had hoped to hear. "All right. Again, I sincerely appreciate it."

As I walked back to Craig's SUV, I flipped through several versions of the story I would tell my guests. Eventually, I landed on something close to the truth.

Restoration. Everyone understood the process of restoring historic homes. And it was only the soft opening. I'd be sure to emphasize what a great rate they were getting and hope that did the trick.

I wanted to call the Sheriff's station and update them with the name of a possible suspect, but it sounded like a visit from Augusta Adams would be far more terrifying than any warning or citation from the local sheriff. There was a lot to learn about living in Misty Meadows, and this might be my first lesson. I'd wait for Augusta's visit and see what transpired.

In the meantime, I should probably finish preparing for my guests. On the way back, I found a shortcut to Moonlight Manor, and my heart swelled with pride when I walked up my wide steps.

All the boxes had been unpacked, but my out-of-place sofa still littered the sitting room. I wanted to keep it in my room on the second level, but I certainly couldn't carry it up multiple flights of stairs by myself. As I pondered the abilities of my ghost team, a soft knock at the front door caught my attention.

I gripped the handle and offered my greeting to Augusta as I opened the door. "That was fast."

The large man on my porch was not Augusta. He was well over six-feet tall, and he was built like a Mack truck. His sandy-blonde hair and soft, green eyes gave more of a teddy bear vibe than convict, but I swallowed loudly. He smiled. "I'm glad you think it was fast. I was worried you'd complain that I didn't show up until afternoon. Mia dropped that list off, but I had to help my dad unload the delivery truck before I headed out to the boondocks on errands. I should be able to get everything on this list taken care of today though, if that's any help?"

"Oh, you're from the hardware store. Sorry, I was expecting Aug—"

"Augusta Adams, for sure. She's the right person to fix that window. I should've introduced myself. I'm Davis Martin." He reached a hand toward me and I struggled to make my limbs move.

"Sure. Right. I'm Sydney. Sydney Coleman. Pleased to meet you." I gripped his hand, but I felt like a child placing her fingers into the paw of a bear.

However, his grip was gentle, and he didn't attempt to exert his masculinity with any sort of overzealous nonsense. He gave me a kind handshake. "Is it all right if I get started, Ms. Coleman?"

"Of course, and please call me Sydney."

He nodded. "Will do." Davis consulted his list, and I stepped out of his way. He didn't ask me for directions, but he seemed to know where he was going. The more I learned about this house, the more

I wondered about its genuine history. Everyone in town seemed to know a heckuva lot more about it than its new owner. At least there were no ghosts roaming around—right now—so that was a plus.

Tapping my fingers on my cheek, I struggled to come up with my own to-do list. As my eyes wandered across the room, they fell on the sofa. Eureka.

"Davis? Davis, are you still on the main floor?" I suddenly wished I had a proper hairdo instead of this messy bun.

A muffled reply came from the kitchen. When I entered, I only saw the lower half of the man. His head, shoulders, and most of his torso were wedged inside a cupboard under the massive kitchen sink.

"I know you're in the middle of something, but I was wondering if I could add one more thing to your list?"

His deep voice echoed from the maple cabinetry. "No problem. What do you need?"

"It's not exactly a repair, but I didn't know where to put the sofa when the movers brought it in, and I definitely need to get it out of the drawing room. Would you be able to help me carry it up to the second level?"

The clanging and scraping of metal on metal were

the only response. I bit my bottom lip and attempted to wait patiently. I hoped I hadn't offended him.

Eventually, the scraping stopped, and he slid out of the cupboard, catching his shirt on the edge and tugging it unceremoniously upward. He wiped some sludgy water from his face and grinned up at me with nothing but confidence. Before I could speak, I had to give myself a little pep talk about keeping it professional and not staring at his bare midriff. Or the muscles he kept there. "You can finish whatever you're doing. And the moving thing is only if you have time."

He reached out his left hand and dropped a couple of large wrenches into his toolbox. "That's item one checked off my list. The leaking J-trap in the kitchen: Fixed. Let me take care of that davenport for you, and then I'll get back to the rest of these items."

"Thank you. Honestly, I really appreciate it." I gestured for him to follow and led the way to my sleek, modern sofa.

He widened his stance and put a hand on his hip. "So this thing is going up to the second floor. Sounds good. Lead the way."

"Yes, way in the rear, on the left." I gazed from him to the sofa and back again. "Do you want me to grab one end?"

"Not necessary. I'll put it on my back and carry it up, like your own personal Sherpa. You just watch the edges and make sure I don't scrape anything important."

"Um, if you say so."

He crouched down, roughly near the middle, and heaved the couch onto his back. His powerful legs pushed upward like some kind of hydraulic press, and he headed for the stairs. I followed behind, keeping him centered and making sure the steel feet on the sofa didn't gouge any of my gorgeous oak or walnut woodwork. When he reached the first landing of the imperial staircase, he paused.

"Do you need to rest, Davis?"

His chuckle was deep and throaty. "Nope. Just tell me if I go left or right."

"Oh, right. No, what I meant was, you're correct. Go left."

He chuckled again and the next time we reached a turn, I paid more careful attention and gave him instructions through the maze of a house to my bedroom.

My bedroom.

Those words made me stumble. It didn't dawn on me until this minute that I was basically inviting this man up to my bedroom. Whoops.

No need to tell him that part. Besides, I assumed he wouldn't think I'd taken a room other than the master suite as my own. No, it was fine. I'd just have him drop off the couch and get back to his list. No big deal.

He turned the last corner, and I thought I detected a slight increase in the pace of his breathing. He wasn't about to let on, but the two-story climb, made with a massive couch on his back, was wearing him down.

"It's this room right here." I held the door wide and guided the sofa through. He crouched, dropped to one knee, and carefully rolled the couch onto its legs. There was a delicate grace about the enormous man.

"Anything else, Ms. Sydney?"

"Please, just Sydney. And no. That was more than enough. If you get through all the other things on that list, I will be seriously indebted."

His eyes scanned the room, and a little color rose to his cheeks. So maybe he did guess. "Well, I better get back downstairs."

"Davis, I don't have any mechanical skills, but I know lots of stuff about websites and social media if I can ever repay the favor."

He paused at the top of the staircase, turned, and

a sly grin lifted one corner of his mouth. "If I'm not mistaken, that box on the counter in the kitchen is from Frannie's place. Can you spare a cupcake?"

I couldn't stop my answering smile. "Oh, I can definitely spare one. But only one. I promised the other to Augusta. I'll be sure to pick up some more before your next visit."

Davis's enormous grin was all the proof I needed that we would definitely be seeing each other again after he finished his work for the day.

always worked the hardest when I thought someone was watching. So rather than stand around looking useless, I headed into the master suite to see what additional cleaning and arranging could be done before the guests arrived.

Everything definitely needed a good dusting. So I opened the large French doors onto the balcony that wrapped around the tower, and beat the dust out of some of the smaller rugs and throw pillows.

Much less dirt than expected—good sign. When I headed back with the large bolster from the end of the massive king-sized bed, I was not alone.

Sir Bogart had taken a position in the middle of the ornate duvet. "It appears you insist on moving forward with the silly notion of guests."

The effort of my housework had produced enough perspiration to cause my straightened hair to curl mercilessly. Plus, there was dust in my contacts and I had no patience for feline drama. "It seems you continue to insist that you're in charge." I tossed the burgundy bolster onto the bed, exactly where he was reclining.

He hissed and scurried out of the way. "You draw a wrath you cannot comprehend my two-legged friend." In a single bound, he leapt to the top of the massive Queen Anne armoire. "Your insolence will not be forgotten, Madam Sydney Coleman." He crouched, curled his tail tightly against his left side, and glared at me through narrow slits for eyes.

"Noted. I'll be sure to remember your total lack of cooperation when we discuss your entertainment."

One eye briefly popped open, but he continued to give me the silent treatment.

Shrugging, I turned my back on His Felineness. A knock at the front door prevented me from offering any additional threats.

I jogged down the stairs. Never let it be said you couldn't teach an old dog new tricks. This time, I waited until I'd fully opened the door before I offered my greeting. "Oh, hi, Augusta. I'm so grateful you were able to fit this into your schedule today."

"Boy, oh boy. That Gladys did a number on this window." She stepped forward, pulled a magnifier from her satchel, and carefully examined the damage. "It's not as bad as it looks. So the Fates smiled on us in that regard. And we continue to make glass from the old local recipes that have been handed down for generations. If I'm not mistaken, I have exact matches for everything except this light, milky-blue color."

"If there's anything I can do, like hunt down a special ingredient or anything, I'm happy to help."

She smiled warmly and leaned forward until her nose touched the glass. "You know what I think? It was quite common for households of this station to include personal items in the recipe. If you don't mind my taking a poke around the old girl, there's a good chance I can figure out if it came from something still on the property."

Since I was eager to move forward with the repair and keep any friends I'd made, I wouldn't mention that I took offense to the phrasing about poking around the girl. "Of course. Help yourself. Davis Martin is here working on some repairs, but other than that, you should have the place to yourself. If you find any locked doors or cupboards, give a shout.

I have a ring full of skeleton keys and no idea what they do."

She gave a matter-of-fact nod and headed into the house.

That signaled the end of our conversation. I marched up to the master suite to continue straightening and add any items to my list that might improve my guest's experience. As I walked past the second portrait gallery, an oil painting of a raven-haired beauty caught my eye.

The sheet which had covered it laid in a pile, roughly, where the woman's feet would have been. The gilt frame shimmered in the dim lighting. Around the fair woman's neck, she wore a beautiful torc. It wasn't made of gemstones; the design appeared to be blown glass. I kept staring at the unique color.

"My mistress was a stunning woman. Was she not?"

The voice gave me goosebumps and I spun in circles trying to find Sir Bogart.

Nothing. I couldn't locate his ghostly form.

Lowering my voice to a barely audible whisper, I hissed, "There are other people in the house. We'll continue our discussion later."

Silence. Hopefully, that was a temporary truce.

I rushed downstairs and called softly to Augusta. I couldn't explain the precise reason, but I had the distinct feeling she was a woman who wouldn't tolerate being hollered at. "Augusta? Augusta? Are you in here?"

"I'm in the drawing room. There's a door, here at the end of this—"

"There's a painting in the gallery that may be worth seeing."

She brushed the dust from her fingers and nodded. "Why don't you see if one of your keys opens this first? An old painting isn't going anywhere."

Fair point. I retrieved my ring of keys from a drawer in the kitchen and rejoined Augusta. "But there's no keyhole. What makes you think it's a door? Maybe it's just the lath and plaster cracking."

Augusta worked her strong fingers along the crease, but there was no latch. I shrugged and turned away, when the voice behind me called out. "Ah ha."

As I spun around to see a section of the wall opened to reveal a steep, narrow staircase. We exchanged excited glances and Augusta gestured for me to lead the way.

"Hold on, I'll grab a flashlight." I returned in a moment and placed a tentative foot on the bottom step.

We ascended in silence.

When I reached the end of the passage, I saw a thin crack of light.

"Feel around for a handle," she suggested.

I used my free hand to check the wall all along the edge. "Nothing."

"Well, give her a good push."

Passing the flashlight to Augusta, I placed both hands on the wall and leaned into it.

The wall itself seemed to creak as it gave way beneath my weight. "It's opening."

The panel swung wide and the two of us tumbled into the burgundy room.

My mouth hung open in awe.

Augusta smiled broadly. "Now that's what I would've expected from Beatrix de Haviland."

"Who?" I turned off the flashlight and stared at the secret passage.

"Beatrix. She was the last living descendant of the original owners of Blodfyss Estate. De Haviland was a stage name."

"She was an actress?"

Augusta shook her head. "She wanted to be an actress, but didn't have the chops. She ended up designing costumes. They say she was a genius with a needle and thread, but her tongue was sharper than her shears. The stories about the raven-haired beauty's flair for the dramatic lived on longer after she'd passed."

When she mentioned the hair, the painting rocketed back to my consciousness. "I think I found something useful in the second portrait gallery—the one that wraps around the spiral staircase."

She gestured for me to lead the way. I rushed toward the painting and looked back to check on Augusta. She made no effort to keep up. Like everyone else in town, she knew exactly where to go.

I pointed to the portrait and the elaborate necklace. "Is that Beatrix?"

Augusta nodded. "Look at that sly grin. That's a woman with many secrets."

The smile seemed to hold a tinge of sadness, but that wasn't important. I pointed to the torc. "Could this be the personal item they used in the glass?" I expected applause, or at least a smile.

Augusta looked at me and shook her head. "Not a chance. Those are elaborate Murano glass beads, likely handmade by the Franchini family. In today's market, that piece of jewelry would be something next to priceless, but even back in her day it would've been far too valuable to grind up." She gazed at the torc in the painting with an artisan's admiration.

"Sorry. I don't know anything about making glass. The color caught my eye, and I thought it could be a match." I picked self-consciously at my nails.

Finally, she smiled. "Tell you what, I'll give you points for heading toward the right turn. If we can identify the origin of that necklace, I can track down the pigment. There's a very good chance it was a color typically chosen by the family."

My eyes brightened. "That's good news, right?"

She rubbed her hands together and rolled her shoulders back and forth. "It's more than I had five minutes ago. Let me finish my pass through the rooms, if that's all right, and if I don't find anything else, that'll be our best lead."

Smiling, I gestured for her to proceed with her search. "If you find any more hidden doors, let me know." I was honestly hoping she would find something on-site to speed up the process, but I was beginning to understand why all those restoration shows on the home improvement networks took twice as long as expected.

In the end, Augusta departed with nothing more than a photo of the long forgotten necklace to guide her search for a matching pigment. Waving as she drove away, my stomach suddenly grumbled for more than cupcakes.

headed around to the side yard to check-in with Davis as the sun sunk low on the western horizon.

He was hanging precariously from a ladder as he clamped and twisted something near the downspout.

I shaded my eyes and looked up at him, ignoring the cut of his pants or the way they hugged his waist. "Hey, I was going to run into town and try to rustle up something to eat. Can I get you anything?"

Davis finished the task at hand, tucked the pliers into his back pocket, and grinned down at me. "Sure. That'd be great. I think I can finish up in about an hour, and it would be awesome if I didn't have to make another trip tomorrow."

Hmmmm. I tried not to be offended by that comment. "Great. Any preference?"

He climbed down the ladder with the speed and finesse of a firefighter. "Not at all." He patted his absolutely ripped abdomen and chuckled. "I pretty much eat whatever I want."

I hoped he couldn't see the jealousy flooding my eyes. "Got it. Back in a flash."

He waved absently and returned to his chores.

As I drove Blue Bell into town, I liked the way it handled. Once I was flush with the money from all the bookings, maybe I could find a used vehicle of the same make and model. I appreciated the hookup from Frannie, and Craig's hospitality, but I knew I couldn't borrow the car forever.

Main Street was deserted at this time of day. Most of the eateries in town must have catered to a breakfast and lunch crowd. I turned and made a second pass. A dim "Open" sign caught my attention, and I pulled to the curb to stare into the window.

Nanita's Mexican food appeared to be my only option. I ordered a chicken taco al carbon for me, and three beef burritos with the works for Davis. I couldn't imagine how much food a man his size could put away, but I didn't want him to think I'd skimped after everything he'd done for me today.

At the last minute, I added a side order of chips and guacamole, and debated whether I should sip a Margarita while I waited. However, I had managed to stay on Sheriff Allen's good side, and I didn't want to push my luck with a possible DUI to ruin my so-far-so-good fresh start.

Before I could ultimately decide, a young waitress brought my food. The to-go bags were brimming with amazing aromas, and I couldn't get home fast enough.

When I pulled the vintage china from the cupboard and arranged the food on the plates, the silly juxtaposition made me giggle. That was the moment Davis walked in.

He inhaled deeply and patted his stomach. "That smells delicious, but is there something I should know?"

My cheeks flushed, and I tipped the refined Bernardaud plate toward him. "No. Just my stupid brain. Something about putting this take-out on fine china made me laugh."

Davis shrugged. "If you ask me, it looks perfect."

I smiled and set the plates, napkins, and silver-ware on the sturdy table in the corner of the kitchen.

He approached the cupboard, opened several doors before he found the glasses, and eventually grabbed two. "Can I get you something to drink, Sydney?"

"I'm afraid we're stuck with water. I haven't had a chance to get to the grocery store."

My thoughtful handyman filled both glasses and brought them to the table. "Water is fine by me. It's important to stay hydrated, that's what I say." He took the chair opposite me, and I pointed to the bags on the counter. "There are two more burritos. So eat up."

We were both pretty hungry and ate in silence. He powered through two burritos before I finished my taco. Davis sighed, leaned back, and wiped his mouth. "I think I'm going to have to call it. Should I put that last burrito in the refrigerator?"

"Sure. Thanks."

As he put the food away, he inhaled sharply.

"What is it?"

He turned toward me with wide eyes. "Do you have a cat?"

"No. Why?" Oh, dear. Sir Bogart was angry with me and apparently he'd decided to take it out on my generous repairman.

"There's a weird old cat toy on the floor. I don't remember seeing it when I grabbed glasses."

I wracked my brain for a plausible explanation. "You probably didn't notice it. I had to grab some keys out of one of these drawers earlier, when Augusta and I were looking for—"

Davis turned toward me. "Maybe, but can you explain how it's moving?" The enormous man looked genuinely terrified as he pressed against the cupboards.

Scraping my chair back, I jumped up and peered around the counter. That darn cat. "You know these old houses. Totally drafty." I lunged forward and grabbed the cat toy in my left hand. "I'll just put this in the drawer and make sure the front door is closed. Did you say you're finished with your list?"

He glanced at the toy in my hand as though it was possessed, and he wasn't entirely wrong. "Um, yeah, almost. I just need to check the light switch in one of the bathrooms on the second floor." His gaze never left the spot on the floor where Sir Bogart had been manipulating the toy.

"Oh, that's the bathroom in the room where you took the sofa."

He edged around the countertop, keeping his distance from me, and the toy.

I shoved it in a drawer and exhaled loudly. "You know what? I bet there's a weird draft coming through the secret passage that Augusta and I found earlier."

At the mention of a secret passage, his entire vibe shifted from terrified to intrigued. "Seriously? I heard the stories about this place when I was a kid. Can you show me?"

At this point, I was willing to do anything to take his mind off the antics of my entitled ghost cat. "Sure. Follow me to the drawing room."

He walked hesitantly behind me, but as soon as he caught sight of the open section of wall, his whole face lit up like a Christmas tree. "It's amazing. Is it all right if I check it out?"

"Of course. Do you want a flashlight?"

He pulled his cell phone from his tool belt and wiggled it back and forth. "I got this. Are you coming?"

"I guess. Lead the way."

When he entered the secret passage, it became incredibly clear that humans of previous generations were significantly smaller than Davis Martin. He had to angle his shoulders sideways just to move up the narrow steps. "It's darker than the inside of my pocket." The light on his phone seemed to be swallowed up before it could do any good.

"There'll be light in a minute."

Augusta and I had left the door at the other end open, and when he saw the proverbial light at the end of the tunnel, he turned off the app on his phone and slipped it back into his tool belt. We were mere steps from the end when the ghost of my butler, Norman, flickered to life at the end of the tunnel.

Davis gasped and, as he twisted in fear, his shoulders wedged. His voice went up an octave, and he shouted, "Did you see that? I swear it was a ghost."

Oh, boy. I was running out of lame explanations. I shoved on one of his shoulders and he slipped forward with a gasp. "I didn't see anything. Honestly, this house has been playing tricks on me all day. I wouldn't worry about it. Let me help you."

"I'd go back down, but I can't turn around," he said.

"It's all right, Davis. I swear, it was nothing."

He inched forward, and I could hear his heartbeat echoing inside the tiny passage. Finally, he burst through the opening into the master suite and paced on the thick carpets. "I'm telling you, I saw the ghost of a butler—or some kind of servant. Are you sure you didn't see it?"

I made every attempt to look innocent. "I didn't. Let's go to the blue room and forget about the light playing tricks in this old house."

He took several deep breaths and his massive shoulders rose and fell like swells in the ocean.

"Yeah. Let's head over to the blue room. I'll focus on what I know and forget about these weird visions, like you said."

Reaching up, I patted him on the back. "That sounds great." When we got to the bedroom tucked in the far wing, I went in first to make sure there were no more spectral surprises. Luckily, the coast was clear. "The bathroom is back this way."

He leaned his phone against the opposite wall on the marble vanity and aimed the light at the switch. "I wish I would've gotten up here before sunset. Is there a lamp, or something we can angle in here to give me some better light?"

"I can run downstairs and grab a flashlight. Would that work?"

His eyes still held a hint of fear. "Um, maybe we can move that lamp." He pointed to a brass floor lamp near the wardrobe.

It didn't take a genius to figure out that big, burly Davis Martin didn't want to be left alone in my little house of horrors. "Sure. We can plug it in right here, and I think the cord will reach into the bathroom."

He nodded, and together we moved the lamp into position. As soon as he had sufficient light, Davis quickly reattached some loose wires behind the faceplate and the delicate sconces on either side of the cerulean-edged mirror glowed to life.

"Thank you. It's actually gorgeous in here."

He glanced around nervously. "Yeah. It's pretty. I better go. My dad will be wondering what happened to me."

I walked him to the front door, thanked him profusely, and even offered to send him home with that last burrito.

He raised his hands and shook his head from side to side. "No. No. You've done enough. You let me know if you come across anything else that needs repair." He waved once and nearly sprinted to his truck.

Great. Just the kind of story I needed circulating around town.

Time to have another chat with my ghostly roommates.

14

As soon as the taillights disappeared down my winding drive, I marched into the house and shouted at the top of my lungs. "Front and center. Norman. Velma. Sir Bogart. Your new mistress demands an audience." My words carried an authority I didn't feel.

Velma was the first to appear. "Yes, miss."

I placed a fist on my hip. "We'll wait for everyone."

Norman appeared next to Velma and Sir Bogart slunk down the imperial staircase with bored disinterest. Once all were present and accounted for, I launched into my speech. "Look, I think we may have gotten off on the wrong foot. It's not too late for us to help each other."

Sir Bogart scoffed and arched his back.

He was going to hear what I had to say, whether he wanted to, or not. "Listen, if you want me to help you, then you're going to have to be less demanding and more gracious. I'm not a rich heiress. I have to work for a living. And if I can't make money, I can't stay here. And if I can't stay here, I can't help you."

Norman bowed slightly. "Yes, madam."

So far, so good. "I have paid guests arriving in two days. There are a ton of things to do to prepare for their arrival. I need all of you to cooperate. Okay?"

The butler and the cook remained silent as they cast their gaze upon the cat. Sir Bogart strutted toward me and struck a regal pose. "The murder of my mistress must be solved. She must be freed from the dark cloud that haunts her. We have already waited decades. Why must we subjugate our needs to yours?"

I rolled my eyes and crouched in front of the pompous feline. "Listen, Bogey."

He twitched his whiskers, but he did not reply.

"I'm not asking anyone to subjugate anything. But here, on the mortal plane, bills have to be paid. I need to get some money coming into this place before I can waltz off and play detective."

He glanced up at Velma and Norman, seemed to nod, and vanished with a crackle of electricity.

I looked everywhere, but saw no sign of Sir Bogart. "Was that agreement? Do we have a deal?" No response came from the ether, but Norman stepped forward. "I shall polish the silver and see that the crystal is spotless, madam."

"Thank you. What about you, Velma? Would you be able to help with the dusting?" She offered a quick curtsy and floated toward the broom closet in the kitchen.

It appeared I'd gotten what I wanted, and I was desperate not to mess it up. Opening the notes app on my phone, I went room to room throughout the manor, making a list of all the little things I planned to handle before the guests checked in.

However, when I reached the third floor, the narrow doorway at the end of the hall called to me once again. I ran down and grabbed a flashlight from the burgundy room and headed up the steep staircase.

The hairs on my arms stood on end, and I felt certain I could hear a voice whispering. I couldn't make out actual words, but as I moved around the attic space, the murmurs grew louder—or softer depending on which direction I moved. My stomach twisted with fear, but my curiosity pulled me onward.

I used the whispers like a compass, guiding me to whatever was in this room. Something called to me, and I needed to make sense of what it was. Better now than when I had guests.

A large trunk in the corner seemed to be the source of the whispers. I unbuckled the thick leather straps and slowly opened the lid. I half expected something to jump out at me, but as soon as the hinges creaked open—the whispering stopped.

Inside the trunk, there were stacks of old newspaper clippings, rolled papers that could be blueprints, and swatches of fabric. I thumbed through the aging collection and unconsciously began separating the items into two piles.

The majority were articles about the acclaimed designs of Beatrix de Haviland, that, and gossip columns mentioning her many suitors. There were awards, citations, and praise from several actors and actresses whom she'd dressed. She'd been accomplished in her profession.

The other stack of clippings mentioned specific starlets, a wealthy director known simply as Armand, movies that had bad reviews, and Edith Plunkett, another designer. She and Beatrix often competed for the job of costumer on the same movies. Though, it seemed Edith rarely beat out Beatrix.

I sorted through these quickly. However, there was something about an engagement announcement that held my rapt attention.

When I flipped through the stack about Beatrix, I found vague mentions of a fiancé. As I searched for a clipping that mentioned a name, my flashlight faded to black. I reached for my phone, but the battery was dead. I frowned at the blank screen. My battery life wasn't what it used to be.

Thin moonlight trickled through the eye-like windows, and I clumsily stumbled back toward the staircase.

What was I doing up here? There wasn't time to get into this. I'd already explained the tight timeline to the ghosts, and here I was, letting myself get distracted by the mystery left behind by the previous mistress of the manor. I had to stay focused and make sure this soft opening was a massive success. My bank account was nearly empty.

Tottering down the dangerous staircase, I hurried to my room and plugged in my phone. Intriguing trunk or not, it was time to get some sleep. I'd have to be up with the sun if I planned on completing my extensive to-do list tomorrow.

Thankfully, I was certain sleep would take me as soon as my head hit the pillow. As the fatigue sunk into my bones, I hastily brushed my teeth and washed my face in the beautiful blue bathroom.

When I hung up the towel and scraped the loose dark hair back from my face, a strange mist covered the bathroom mirror. It was as though someone had taken a steamy shower and fogged the surface. But when I tried to wipe it away, my hand seemed to disappear into the smoky surface.

The cold mist pulled me deeper, and I struggled to free my hand.

Darkness swallowed me, and once again I felt the satin lining of the coffin pressing against my skin. I banged against the domed lid and called out for help.

Bolting upright, I woke with a scream. My room was bathed in silvery moonlight and I had no memory of climbing into the massive bed. Cold sweat trickled down my back. I couldn't possibly fall back asleep.

Heading down to the kitchen to heat up some of the hot chocolate Frannie had sent over, I pushed on every light switch as I went. The path of light helped keep shadows at bay, and the terror of the dream faded as I rubbed my eyes.

"Wow. I must've been way more exhausted than I

thought." I'd hoped one of my spirit roommates would answer, but the only response was the eerie quiet of the vast mansion.

In the kitchen, I busied myself lighting the stove, and pouring hot chocolate into a small saucepan.

Note to self: Get a microwave as soon as possible.

The whole gas stove thing was a newly acquired skill. I grew up with a cheap electric range and wasn't entirely sure what I was doing with actual flames. So, once I smelled something close to burning, I took the pan off the flame and clumsily poured the steaming liquid into a mug.

Velma appeared, looking flustered. "Oh, miss, you should've called me. Let me take care of that pot." She swooshed through me, instantly unsettling the calming effects of the warm cocoa, and clattered the pan into the sink.

Slumping into a chair at the table, I sipped the elixir in silence. Once she dried the pan and returned it to the hook, she bobbed her head in my direction. "Is there anything else I can get you, miss?"

"Velma, has anyone else lived here? Since your mistress?"

She glanced left and right, and I half expected Sir Bogart to appear and either tell her to bite her tongue, or perhaps give her permission to speak. When no one came to her aid, she stumbled through an answer. "A few, miss. But none stayed as long as you."

As long as me? I'd only been here a couple of nights. "Did any of them mention having bad dreams?"

A flash of guilt flickered through the apparition. "I think— I think they all have 'em, miss."

"Did you ever hear anyone say what the bad dreams were about?"

"No, miss. Can't say as I did."

As I sipped my hot chocolate, I struggled to come to terms with telling my troubles to a ghost. Although, who was she going to tell? "I've had the same dream, twice. I'm trapped inside a coffin—"

She zoomed toward me and gripped my shoulders. "That's the trouble, miss. That's what happened to Mistress Beatrix. We all felt it, but there's nothing we can do. Bogey figures she's trapped in between here and there. He says the only way to set her free is to clear her name."

"What do you mean 'clear her name?' " A strange memory trickled in, and I recalled the cat saying something about freeing his mistress. "Was Miss de Haviland accused of a crime?"

"No. They said she— the coppers—Well, they..."

"What is it, Velma? You can tell me anything."

"They said it was a suicide." Velma dabbed at her tears with the corner of her apron.

"Can you be sure it wasn't? The police must've based that on the evidence. What makes you think they were wrong?"

"She had everything, our mistress, and she would never— I ain't religious, but Mistress Beatrix was devout. She'd never take her own life, miss."

The warm liquid was finally doing its duty, and sleep tugged at my eyelids. "We'll talk about this again soon, Velma. I promise, but I have to get some sleep. I have so much to do tomorrow."

She drifted to a standing position and gripped her hands behind her back. "Yes, miss."

I stumbled upstairs and pulled the blankets onto my out-of-place leather sofa. Something about that bed, and the recent nightmare, made my skin crawl. The house seemed to have a mind of its own, but I was determined to prove that I was stronger than any rumors, superstitions, or ghost stories.

15

heck-in day had finally arrived. Making a third, or maybe tenth, pass through the burgundy room, I tugged at the corners of the duvet, re-fluffed the pillows, and straightened picture frames. I knew how important this first impression would be, and I was willing to do whatever it took to make sure my guests enjoyed the stay of a lifetime.

As I brushed a speck of dust from the antique music box on the dresser, Norman popped into the visual spectrum beside me. "Anything I can do to assist, madam?" "Would you like me to bring their bags up when they arrive?"

"Norman. You can't be doing that. And I don't just

mean to me. You can't be interacting with other humans, especially not with my guests."

Norman wasn't the worst of my worries though, not by a long shot.

I marched to the first landing on the imperial staircase, took a deep breath, and boomed out a general announcement that would put even Mia's voice to shame. "Attention all disembodied apparitions, spirit world specters, and ghosts in general. Under no circumstances are you allowed to talk to, appear to, or pester the guests."

Otherworldly silence.

"I'll take your silence as agreement." I trudged down the steps and fussed with the large flower arrangement that adorned the round table in the grand entrance. Yes, it was an extravagance. I was pretty much putting all my eggs into the first impression basket. My bed-and-breakfast debut had to make a splash or the whole endeavor would fail. At the bottom of the stairs, I paused. Was I forgetting something? Perhaps something important?

"Fiddlesticks," I mumbled to myself when I realized what it was. Frannie had given me specific instructions to place the fresh chocolate chip cookies in the oven at a low temperature for ten minutes. She assured me that there wasn't any situation that couldn't be fixed with warm chocolate chip cookies. Plus, the scent would be incredibly inviting to the guests as they arrived.

I scurried into the kitchen and carefully laid the scrumptious cookies on a tray. The oven heated up quickly, so I covered the tray with a clean dish towel and popped it in.

There. It would smell like heaven in here in no time.

A deep bass chiming filled the ground floor. My new doorbell heralded all the hopes and dreams I had for this place.

As I hurried toward the front entrance, I checked my hair in a hallway mirror. It was no New York City salon hair-day, but in Maine and on a budget, compromises had to be made.

I gripped the brass door handle, pasted on a megawatt smile, and swung the door open with a flourish. "Good afternoon. Welcome to Moonlight Manor." Sweeping my arm wide, I gestured for them to enter.

However, before they crossed the threshold, the husband glanced at the board in the window frame and frowned. "Anything we should know about?"

Don't worry, I'd been practicing my answer to this one for days. "Not at all. Unfortunately, the clumsy movers cracked it and the only place in town that could restore the vintage stained glass said it would take weeks for the color-matched glass to arrive."

He grumbled, but nodded and entered.

"You can leave your bags here and I'll have them brought up to your room. You're in our largest suite, the burgundy room. Let me show you up." Neither of them so much as glanced at the gorgeous floral arrangement.

I led the way to the master suite and opened the French doors onto their private terrace. As I turned to drop a couple of interesting historical facts, the wife scampered over and closed the doors. "It's quite drafty. I don't want to catch cold on our first day."

Wow. This was going to be a lot harder than I'd imagined. Deep breaths. "Will you be needing a restaurant recommendation for dinner?"

The husband stared at me. "I thought all the meals would be served here."

I resisted the urge to explain to him that breakfast was a morning meal, and instead dug deep into my marketing bag of tricks and steadied my voice. "Dinner isn't part of your package, Mr. Griffin, but I'd be happy to provide something for you this evening and make reservations for you tomorrow night."

Once again, he grumbled under his breath.

"That'll be fine. My wife has nut allergies, and I am allergic to gluten and shellfish."

Shellfish. Who comes to Maine—I had to scold myself mentally and keep silently chanting, *These are my guests. Their wants and needs are more important than my own.* "Not a problem. I'll make sure the cook is informed of all your dietary preferences."

Boy, I hoped Craig wouldn't hold it against me when he found out my first guests wouldn't be enjoying any of his delicious *lobstahs.*

Mrs. Griffin straightened her sweater and shook her head. "They are not preferences, young lady. They are allergies that could land myself or my husband in the hospital—in dire straits."

There was no way in all of heaven and earth that I would ask these crabapples to leave a review. "Understood. Let me get your bags." I hustled out of the room before either of them could make any further disparaging remarks.

Putting a pin in the valet duties, I searched through the pantry, refrigerator, and the gift basket from Frannie. Everything had a consistent theme.

Breakfast.

Guess I better run into town and pick up supplies. I'd have to call Frannie on the way and see if I could convince her to pull a night shift.

Steering with one hand, I placed the call. "Frannie? Hey, it's Sydney. I hate to say it, but my premiere guests could be my last. They are absolutely the worst. For some reason, they assumed ALL their meals would be served at the manor, and they're insisting on supper. But that's only one of the problems."

We both chuckled as she pointed out my lack of advanced cookery skills.

"The other problem is I have nothing to serve them. I'm headed into town, and I could sure use some pointers. Also, I know you're probably tired of being paid in smiles . . . But is there any chance you can pull a night shift?" Frannie said she would text me foolproof recipes and a shopping list, but she had to make a special batch of muffins for the Chamber of Commerce mixer, which started at 7:00 a.m. tomorrow.

"I totally understand. Send me what you've got, and if you say it's foolproof, I'll cross my fingers and hope I'm not too big a fool."

By the time I got to the local Hannaford's, Frannie's tips and list had arrived. I carefully purchased each and every item, and paid for the groceries with one of my credit cards that still had a smidge of room.

When I returned to the property, Mr. Griffin was

banging his suitcases up the stairs, grumbling—shocker—under his breath.

Dropping the bags of groceries on the parquet floor, I hurried toward him. "I do apologize, Mr. Griffin. I had to run to town to grab some items for tonight's supper. Let me get these."

He didn't even look at me. "I've taken them this far. I can make it the rest of the way. You should probably see what's burning."

Burning?

"Oh, *Grapes of Wrath*." I ran into the kitchen, grabbed an oven mitt and pulled the tray of mostly blackened, former chocolate chip cookies from the oven. The tray clattered to the counter as I yanked my hand out of the old potholder to suck on my burned finger. Of course, I'd found the only hole in the oven mitt.

"One disaster after another. At this rate, the ghosts will be the least of my worries." I surveyed the kitchen and exhaled loudly. At least there was no smoke. No fantastic cookie smell either, but no smoke. Thank heaven for small favors. I tipped the burned discs into the waste bin and angrily tossed the tray into the enormous white sink.

Crossing my arms over my chest, I glared at the traitorous tray. "I'll deal with you later."

The groceries wouldn't bring themselves into the kitchen, so I returned to the foyer and collected the three bags. I had no idea how long it would take me to stumble through these supposedly foolproof recipes, so I unpacked the supplies and tried to get organized.

While I was busy looking up the term *julienne* online, Velma drifted out of the pantry. "Anything I can do, miss?"

I threw my hands in the air and sighed helplessly. "You know what? Yes. I give up. I don't know the first thing about real cooking, and I'm supposed to make a delicious dinner for these unbelievably picky, incredibly uptight guests. So, yes. I'd love some help."

Velma floated along the large center island and examined my ingredients. "It looks like you're making chicken and rice, with minted peas. Is that right, miss?"

Wow, even a ghost was handier in the kitchen than me.

"Yes. It's a combination of wild rice and brown rice, and the chicken breasts are supposed to be browned and then added to the rice or something." I rubbed my hand across my forehead.

"Do you have a recipe card, miss?" Velma

adjusted her apron and clasped her small, strong hands at her waist.

Turning my phone toward her, I showed her the picture of the recipe Frannie had sent.

She gazed into the glowing device and poked at it with her ethereal finger as she continued to marvel at the luminous words. "That ain't like no paper I've ever seen. If you read it off to me, miss, I'll get started. We should have supper on by six, if that suits you."

My shoulders relaxed a fraction of an inch, and I smiled. "That sounds wonderful."

"Which chicken did you want butchered, miss?" She picked up the cleaver and smiled calmly.

My whole body shivered. "What? No. No butchering." I pushed the packet of chicken toward her. "You use these chicken breasts from the market."

Velma stared at the plastic-wrapped packet. "I prefer fresh, but if you insist, miss."

My heart pounded at the thought of how they bought chicken during pre-ghost Velma's life. "Yes, please."

"As you wish, miss."

I took a seat at the oak table in the corner and read aloud the remaining ingredients and measurements to Velma. She was a wizard in the kitchen. Any time I asked her a question, she patiently answered or demonstrated. It was like having cooking lessons from my own private chef. Maybe living in the haunted manor wasn't going to be as bad as I thought? If this dinner turned out as delicious as it seemed, there was a chance I could win the Griffins over and get them to leave a brief positive review.

Time was slipping by and Velma had made stunning progress. I even helped by preparing the salad. It wasn't much, but I felt I'd contributed something. Covering the large salad bowl in plastic wrap, I placed it in the fridge. Maybe I should head up and let the Griffins know what time their supper would be served. When I turned to walk out of the kitchen, I came face to face with a horrified Mrs. Griffin.

"That colander is floating in midair."

I glanced to my left and saw Velma rinsing the fresh peas under the sink. I raced over and grabbed the strainer from her hands. "Oh, this? I just had it balanced on another bowl. Trying to multitask, you know."

Mrs. Griffin shook her head and pulled her sweater tight around her. "I know what I saw. It was floating." She stepped backward, her face a mask of fear.

"I'm sure it looked very strange. I was about to

come up to let you and Mr. Griffin know that supper will be served at six. We'll be having a salad of fresh local ingredients, minted peas, arroz con pollo, and a fresh fruit gelato for dessert course."

Mrs. Griffin shook her head. "We don't eat strange foreign foods."

Of course they don't. I could barely restrain my eye roll. "It's only chicken and rice, Mrs. Griffin. I assure you there's nothing foreign. All locally sourced, organic ingredients."

She backed out of the kitchen and continued to mumble, "I know what I saw," under her breath.

I had to stop getting my hopes up. These two were a lost cause. If I could simply make it through the rest of the weekend without one of them calling the police, that would be the only win I could hope for.

16

'd like to spare you the details of the, according to the Griffins, undercooked, over seasoned, disappointingly plated dinner. Not even a floating colander could salvage their opinion of it.

Honestly, I couldn't get them back upstairs fast enough. And after I took them extra towels, hot tea, and another blanket, the Griffins finally retired for the evening.

I texted Frannie a heartfelt thank you for her amazing dinner suggestions and placed the blame for the meal's failure squarely on my shoulders.

Velma had done a magnificent job, and everything had been spectacular. I'd eaten at the finest restaurants in the Big Apple, and there was no fault in the dishes we'd served. The simple truth was, the

Griffins could not be pleased. I'd dealt with clients like that back at the Aconite Agency.

We'd put together two or three stunning creative presentations, but the potential clients would always find something to complain about. Of course, losing a client here or there hardly mattered to such a successful agency. For me, failing to impress the Griffins could have dire consequences for my future bookings.

I lay on the cream-colored sofa and pulled the blankets around me. Maybe breakfast would be the ticket. Frannie's creations certainly—

"Fiddlesticks." Mr. Griffin is gluten-free. The thought of dietary restrictions hadn't even occurred to me when I approved Frannie's menu. Delicious bacon and onion mini quiches, fresh banana walnut muffins, Dijon-mustard-glazed bacon rolls, and Maine blueberries would never make the cut. My guest couldn't even eat the star of the meal, which was absolutely the quiche. I'd eaten three at the taste test.

Hopefully, some amazing solution would come to me during the night. Struggling to find the path to dreamland, my eyelids finally succumbed.

With no idea how much time had passed, a blood-curling scream ripped me from my dreamless slumber.

I ran through the halls toward the burgundy room and nearly crashed directly into the fleeing Mrs. Griffin. "I know what I saw." She tugged at her dressing gown and raced toward the imperial staircase.

"Mr. Griffin, what happened?"

He yanked the handle up from his rolling suitcase and glared at me. "I'm not sure if these theatrics are part of the Unforgettable Weekend package, but I can assure you we do not find them amusing." He marched past me and his shoulder jostled me rudely.

"Mr. Griffin, what are you talking about?"

He paused but did not bother to face me. "There was frost on the mirror in the bathroom, and my wife claimed to see the reflection of a dark-haired woman floating behind her. I will not tolerate this type of nonsense. We did not come here to be frightened or have some sort of paranormal experience. You've made a grave error, young lady. I am the editor for the most popular travel magazine in the eastern United States. I shall be writing a scathing piece on this horrible establishment."

And with that, Mr. and Mrs. Griffin rolled out of my doomed business venture and loaded into a taxi.

I crept up the stairs to my room, collapsed onto the couch, and sobbed.

"Such behavior is unbecoming a woman of your talents, Miss Coleman." The feline voice took me by surprise.

Swiping at the tears on my face, I struggled to focus on the pulsating glow that became Sir Bogart, uncertain I could bear another round of criticism right now. "I told you, I needed the money. I can't believe all of you would sabotage my bed-and-breakfast like this. If there's no money, there's no—anything." I buried my face in my hands and resumed feeling sorry for myself.

Sir Bogart sauntered toward me and shook his head. "I explained to you how it would be a terrible idea to have guests. I mentioned in great specificity that the murder of my mistress must first be solved."

Anger quickly replaced sadness, and I slammed my hand down on the couch cushion. "Listen, you ungrateful demon cat, I don't care about your mistress. She killed herself. Not my problem. Figuring out how to save this disastrous soft opening from imploding—that's my problem."

His Felineness eased onto his haunches and shook his head like a disappointed schoolmaster. Behind him a blackness swirled into oblivion and a woman in green appeared. Her ghostly fingers reached toward me, and her eyes burned with vengeance. Her bright-red lips moved but no voice penetrated the void. I stared in horror, but the lips seemed to say, *Help me.* And suddenly the swirling blackness vanished.

Sir Bogart seemed to arch an eyebrow as he waited for my response.

"What was that?"

"My mistress."

"Is she the one— Is she sending me these nightmares?"

Sir Bogart nodded. "She is trapped between the mortal plane and the spirit world. Not earthbound as me and my companions. She cannot take corporeal form or move physical objects. However, she has perfected the use of chilling air, dark dreams, and recently she has gained the ability to appear for brief moments." He sighed and hung his head. "Oh, how I miss her."

The truth was stranger than fiction. Norman, Velma, and Sir Bogart hadn't interfered. The blame all fell on Beatrix de Haviland. How had I ended up in a haunted manor, tasked with solving a decades-old death?

I took a breath. "Okay, I'm sorry I blamed you for

the mess with Mr. and Mrs. Griffin. I want to help. Honestly, if she was murdered, I'd love to figure out who did it. But I'm absolutely out of money, and this alleged murder happened over seventy years ago. The universe seems to sustain you, but I cannot depend on anyone but me. So, unless there's a stash of gold bars under this house, I've got to make this bed-and-breakfast thing work." I drew a ragged breath and continued. "I can try to work on the case at the same time, but money coming in has to be the priority. Do you understand?"

The large, majestic cat lifted his head and seemed almost to smile. "You shall need your ring of keys, milady. Follow me."

Snatching the ring of keys from my dresser, I followed the sleek muscular cat down to the ground floor and into the corner of the kitchen behind the sturdy oak table.

Sir Bogart raised onto his hind legs and scratched a singular claw at a spot on the wall.

I frowned down at the ghostly feline. "Hey, if you damage the lath and plaster, I'll have to pay for a repair. What did I just tell you about our money situation?"

Sir Bogart didn't bother answering. Instead, he kept pawing at whatever had caught his attention.

In a moment, an oddly shaped patch of darkness appeared. The keys rattled in my hand as I leaned down closer in the moonlight. The spot resembled a keyhole. "Is that—?"

He turned toward the key ring in my hand, and out of the dozens of strange skeleton keys now within his reach, gripped one between his teeth and held it up toward me.

When I took it from him, I straightened, and the hairs on my arms stood on end. "Please tell me this will not lead to a dungeon. Or more haunting. I'm not sure I can handle another specter in my house."

Bogey snickered in that strange, rattling way. "Hardly. But if it is money you seek, this may provide a remedy for your lack."

"Well, what are we waiting for?" I pushed the key into the lock and turned. As with the other hidden doors, a section of the wall eased outward, and I dragged it backward. While the keyhole had been within Sir Bogart's reach, the door itself was large enough for me to step through without crouching. The hinge mechanisms on this secret panel was well maintained. There was no struggle, and almost no sound.

Reaching inside the darkened opening, I found the buttoned light switch. To my great relief, the light snapped on with the first push. It illuminated a stairway before me, and I swallowed hard as I stepped onto the first tread. "Swear on your mistress that this isn't a trap."

Sir Bogart's furry brow wrinkled. "We are in this together now, Miss Coleman. And for all intents and purposes, you are now my mistress."

The statement hardly comforted me, but I crept down the staircase all the same. Few steps creaked, but each one startled me enough I had to bite back each whimper. At the bottom, I felt around for a second light switch. When the three caged bulbs sprang to life, my heart nearly stopped beating. "Oh, my—."

Sir Bogart strutted ahead of me and grinned slyly over his shoulder. "Not exactly gold bars, but they should fetch a handsome price."

The wine cellar, buried beneath the ballroom, that lay before me hadn't been touched since the death of Beatrix de Haviland. I moved reverently down the dusty rows and could barely contain my glee. Some of these bottles were hundreds of years old. If I could find the proper auction house and sell only the most valuable bottles, I would be able to pay off my debts, keep this place afloat, and possibly afford to have the gardens properly updated.

Sinking to my knees on the floor, I attempted to stroke the semi-corporeal cat. "Sir Bogart, I know we got off on the wrong foot. But I don't know how to thank you. You saved me. You saved all of us."

He turned toward me and nuzzled his silken head against my hand. "Would milady perchance have a string?"

Shrugging my shoulders, I tilted back on my heels. "I'm sure I can find one. Why?"

He grinned up at me. "I would so enjoy a brief bit of entertainment."

"Oh, Bogey. I'm all over it."

17

The meeting with the appraiser from one of New York's finest auction houses went well. It wasn't the smashing success I had envisioned, but it was enough.

He carefully examined the contents of the wine cellar and discovered five rare bottles. The rest of the collection could be sold for anywhere from one to three hundred dollars per bottle. Something to keep in mind, but not worth the trouble or expense of the auction house.

However, the five bottles he accepted for auction were—an 1810 Tres Cortados; a Millennium Port 1880 Colheita; a 1900 Grande Champagne Cognac; a 1940 Niepoort Garrafeira Port; and a 1950 Chateau

Cheval Blanc St. Emilion Grand Cru—and would fetch a possible total of $20,000 at auction.

He put his offer and his recommendation in writing, and I accepted. Then he pressed his business card into my palm and left with the bottles as quickly as he had come, promising to keep me updated as the auction progressed.

It wasn't the bar of gold windfall I'd hoped would clear all of my debts and pave the way for a happily ever after, but it would keep me afloat, and that was all that mattered right now.

Good thing, too. Because when Mr. Griffin's article hit the online travel world, it instantly went viral. The rest of my bookings were canceled within forty-eight hours of the article's release, and the incident nearly snuffed out my little flame of hope.

At least the wine money would keep the lights on until we came up with Plan B. In the meantime, with the impending auction lessening the financial pressure of the way forward, I agreed to get to work on Beatrix de Haviland's murder case. Sir Bogart was smugly satisfied with my change in heart.

Though, a minor detail troubled me in a major way: I had about as much experience being a detective as I had being a chef. And being an inexperienced chef hadn't gone so well. The one thing I had going for me was the current otherworldly residents of the manor. They provided direct access to three people—well, two people and a talking cat—that were alive on the night Beatrix was supposedly murdered. It seemed like the best place to start would be to question them.

Later, heading into the kitchen, I grabbed a chair and opened the note app on my phone. I spoke to the empty room, knowing the cook could hear me. "Velma, I wanted to talk to you about the night Miss de Haviland was killed. You must've cooked for the party, right?"

Velma appeared, flitting nervously about the kitchen and wringing her hands. "Yes, miss. But there's a little thing you don't know."

"There are a ton of things I don't know, Velma. But you were here at the manor that night, weren't you?"

"Yes, miss. But I died that night, too."

Part of me understood Velma's sentiment. "I'm sure you all felt like you died a little when your mistress was taken from you. Now I need to hear what you remember about the guests and who you saw your mistress talking to."

"That's just the thing, miss. She didn't have the chance to talk to anyone. She were about to make her grand entrance down the main stairs, and that horrible Miss Plunkett woman came in on the arm of Sir Armand, and milady ran up to her room and refused to come out."

I glanced up from my phone. "She didn't attend her own party?"

"No, miss. I made her some tea and took it upstairs. But when I set the tray down outside her door to fetch my key, someone smashed me on the back of the head with a candlestick."

I gasped. "What? You were murdered on the same night as Beatrix?"

"As I said, miss."

"Oh, my." Some part of me had forgotten that a requirement of ghost-hood was death. The information went into the notepad on the app. "Velma, murdered same night," I murmured.

"Yes, miss. That's what I'm saying." She tugged at her apron and shook her head.

"So, who hit you with the candlestick? You must've seen them when you came out of your body. Isn't that how these things work?" I couldn't be sure, since I'd never died, but it was my best guess.

She pressed a hand to the back of her head and

winced. "Well, miss, I fell down and I don't remember nothing, but I don't think I died right away. Because by the time I were a ghost, someone had moved my body to the bottom of the stairs and dumped out the tea tray."

"What? Someone staged another accident? I can't believe the police bought that. Two mysterious deaths in one house on the same night." I stood from the chair and paced beside the butcher-block counter. Why had none of the investigating officers thought it strange to have two fatal accidents in the same night?

Velma nodded in agreement. "That's right. They said my mistress killed herself, and I must've rushed off to call for a doctor and fell myself. It were nonsense, o' course. There weren't nothing I could do about it. I couldn't pick things up or talk to people like I can now. It took me ages to learn."

I attempted to pat her on the back, but the sensation of my hand seeping into her energy gave me the willies. "It's not your fault, Velma. Someone killed Beatrix, and they must've killed you as well."

She shrugged. "Can't imagine why. I never bothered nobody in my life."

Tapping my fingers on my lip, I reviewed the possibilities. "Maybe they thought you saw something or overheard something. Are you sure you didn't?"

"No, miss. Nothing."

"All right, thanks for telling me. I better talk to Norman. Do you know where I might find him?"

She vanished with a strange pop, and a moment later, Norman appeared. He inclined his head. "Cook says you need to speak with me, madam."

"Yes. I only just found out that Velma was killed the same night as Beatrix. Did you also die at that party?"

He shook his head. "No, madam. Our mistress left everything to Sir Bogart in her will. The staff was most displeased. The lot of them packed their bags, some pilfering objects as they left, and departed the manor in the days following the deplorable events." He cleared his throat and continued. "The party was meant to announce our mistress's engagement to Sir Armand. However—"

"But he showed up with Edith Plunkett on his arm. No wonder Beatrix was so upset."

Norman pressed his hands together in front of him and nodded. "It was a most unfortunate turn of events. After her death, I chose to accept the small salary that was offered to the staff person who would care for Sir Bogart. I had always found him an amiable feline, and I felt I owed it to our mistress." He sniffled and looked away.

"Owed her for what?"

"If I'd been at my post instead of fetching bottles from the wine cellar, perhaps the tragedies would not have occurred." He avoided my eyes and straightened his vest.

"You don't know that, Norman. What if they killed you, too? You can't blame yourself for the actions of a depraved murderer."

He sighed. "Perhaps not. In the dark days that followed, I discovered, through the twisted paths of gossip, that Miss Plunkett had trapped Sir Armand with a pregnancy. She had arranged a servant to discover them in a compromised situation, and when she announced she was with child, his family was forced to legitimize the heir."

"That dirty scoundrel. I mean Edith, not the guy. Beatrix must've been heartbroken."

Norman nodded. "I served our mistress with honor, madam. But if you'd permit me to speak freely?"

Tilting my head, I nodded. "Of course. Speak as freely as you like."

"Our dear Miss de Haviland had an unkind side. She so loved the spotlight and the attention of wealthy gentlemen, and she wasn't above a well-placed bribe or stolen kiss."

I didn't have the heart to explain to Norman how the dating world had devolved since the days of Beatrix de Haviland, but I appreciated his honesty. "So you're saying she may have had more enemies than just Edith Plunkett?"

He inhaled sharply. "I hesitate to call them enemies, madam. However, she had perhaps caused offense to more than a handful of men and women in the upper echelons of society. Persons of means. Well-equipped for retaliation."

Nodding, I knew exactly what he meant. "I found some clippings in the attic, but they all pointed to an intense rivalry with Edith Plunkett. Was there anyone else you could think of?"

He sighed, and I could see that it broke his heart a little to reveal the secrets of his previous mistress. Despite how necessary the divulgence was, in light of my attempt at an investigation.

"If you'll follow me, madam."

Norman silently led me up to the third level. He walked past the servants' rooms without turning his head. When he reached the small studio at the end, he held the door and gestured for me to enter. Norman floated in behind me and secured the door. "Velma doesn't know about this. Of course, I've shown Sir Bogart, but he's not sure how to proceed."

With that, he opened a shallow desk drawer and removed a thin, red journal. He placed it on the desk and carefully leafed through the yellowed pages.

"Where did that come from?" I moved toward him and pointed at the open pages.

He cleared his throat and sighed. It was a long mournful sound, more like a moan that stretched across the ages. "It is the final journal of my former mistress. The letter they found on the desk in the burgundy room had been written on a page torn from this very book. Whoever wrote the message had pressed quite firmly. I was able to make a rubbing of the original note."

Norman turned the book toward me and I solemnly read the suicide letter supposedly written by Beatrix.

Dear ones, I fear the pain of losing my precious Armand is too much. There is no award or role that can replace him in my heart. I fear I must drop the curtain and bring this final scene to a close. I know I shall never love another this deeply again. My solicitor holds my last will and testament. He shall see that my affairs are handled properly. My only regret is that I haven't time to make my own gown for the funeral. I should like to wear the red and gold frock which I created for Marilyn Russell. It, too, deserves

death. All my love to my sweet and loyal Bogey,
Beatrix

I touched the page reverently and smiled at
Norman. "Thank you for sharing that with me. It
seems clear from this note that she fully intended to
commit suicide. Why do you doubt the police find-
ings and suspect murder?"

Norman grumbled. "The gala was to herald her
engagement to Armand, and she'd worked tirelessly
on the finest gown ever created. She was found in the
burgundy room in her glorious green garment,
madam. However, there was a cheap flower pinned to
her bodice. That was not in keeping with my
mistress's impeccable styling."

What he said made some sense. Though, this
letter didn't seem to support his doubts about the
results of the investigation. I studied the face of the
hovering man. He believed everything he said, and I
didn't intend to let any of them down.

"All right. I didn't know the woman, but I believe
you. However, the single fact that she had a tacky
corsage hardly seems enough to go on. Maybe it had
sentimental meaning? If it wasn't suicide, there has
to be another suspect or two. You said she didn't have
enemies, but you admitted she'd angered powerful
people. Maybe those powerful people could afford to

hire someone to exact their vengeance. Don't you think?"

He frowned. "Perhaps. However, there is the matter of the poison."

"She died by taking poison?"

The butler shook his head. "That was the belief of the investigating officer. There was some liquid in a crystal glass on her vanity, next to the note. It was shown to have contained arsenic."

I sighed and lifted my hands helplessly. "I hate to say it, but that seems to support the suicide theory."

Norman drifted aimlessly across the studio and shook his head. "I must disagree. My mistress always wore the most lovely victory-red lipstick. She applied it the moment she got out of bed in the morning. I don't think a single member of her staff, and certainly not a single acquaintance, had ever seen her without it."

"And was she wearing the lipstick that night?"

He nodded fiercely. "Indeed, madam. That's the problem."

I wasn't exactly following Norman's logic. If his mistress always wore the same lipstick, and she was wearing lipstick that night, I couldn't understand which part didn't make sense. "Sorry, I don't follow your meaning."

Norman clasped his hands behind his back, ceased his drifting, and fixed me with a pleading stare. "I saw the glass, before the officer removed it. There was no lipstick on the rim. Not the faintest smudge." He cleared his throat. "I'm no expert, but it seems unlikely that a woman could drink from an exquisite piece of crystal stemware and not leave the slightest hint of her lip color."

"All right. That's something. What about this note? Why would she have written a suicide note if she didn't plan to kill herself?"

Norman's aura brightened, once I agreed to accept one of his observations as cause for doubt. "On that, I have two theories. The first being my mistress did, in fact, not write the note. If someone had access to her journal, they could've mimicked her hand, at least enough to fool the clumsy coppers who managed this farce of an investigation. And—" He floated toward the book and again paged delicately through the folios. "To understand my second theory, you must have a look at these previous entries."

I approached the desk and glanced at the page where Norman's ethereal finger pointed. When I read the words, they had a familiar and disconcerting ring.

Dear ones, I've lost the position of costumer on The Golden Sphinx. The sly and deceitful Edith Plunkett somehow influenced the director. I fear she may be gaining ground with my fabric supplier as well. I cannot face the world after this horrible failure. There is no hope and no better textile manufacturer. I fear I must end this scene before it's time. I call Fin. The curtain must fall. To my terribly spoiled Bogey, I leave my love. The solicitors will take care of the rest. Adieu, your Bea

"Is this a practice note?" I pointed to the page in confusion.

Norman shook his head and gestured toward the date.

When I looked back at the rubbing, this supposed suicide note had been written two years earlier. I looked into Norman's glowing eyes and shrugged. "I don't understand."

He carefully paged through the book and showed me three or four additional "suicide notes." His ghostly gaze bored into mine. "My mistress was a passionate, creative woman. She celebrated her wins with great gusto and mourned her losses with the desolation of the forsaken. It was the way of her."

I thought back to the moment when Lucas had tipped his hand. If I'd kept a journal, and written down my feelings at that precise moment, who knows what I would've penned? A part of me had felt my life had ended, and I might be death-doomed. In the passion of the moment, maybe I would've thought that ending it all was the only solution. Truth rang within Norman's sentiment. Perhaps I understood Beatrix de Haviland better than I imagined.

18

The information Norman had shared sent my thoughts spinning. I wandered down the stairs and found myself turning the garnet-glass handle of the burgundy room.

As I gazed at the antique furnishings, I tried to imagine Beatrix in this room.

Did she take her own life? Velma said the door had been locked. She had to set the tray down to fetch her key. But if she was killed before Beatrix, the murderer could've taken Velma's key, entered the room, killed Beatrix, and secured the door after they left.

No. There was a house full of people and whoever killed Velma took the time to arrange her body on the stairs to make it look like an accident. They wouldn't have risked leaving her in the hallway to be discovered.

Pacing across the richly detailed Persian carpet, I stared at the vanity where Beatrix may have written her final, true suicide note.

What about Bogey? By all accounts, he was the only thing she valued more than fame. He must've been in the room.

"Sir Bogart? Bogey, I need to talk to you."

He appeared, quite suddenly, in the middle of the deep-maroon and gold duvet. He groomed the glistening fur on his left foreleg and ignored me.

I jumped straight into an explanation, hoping he'd pay attention once he identified the topic. "I'm looking into the possible murder, like you asked, but some things don't make sense."

Sir Bogart stretched leisurely and flopped onto his side. "They do not. Which is why I require your assistance."

"I talked to Velma, and Norman showed me the journal. The thing—"

Sir Bogart was on his feet in a flash. "You've seen the journal?"

"Yes. And I think I understand why you all suspect murder. It seems like Beatrix had a habit of overreacting and writing suicide notes, even though she had no intention of actually killing herself. She had a flare for the dramatic."

Bogey's eyes brightened. "Exactly. The suicide note was all part of the hoax. Norman has always had a sharp eye."

I nodded my agreement and sat on the edge of the bed. "What do you remember?"

The feline apparition flickered painfully, and I worried he would disappear altogether.

"Bogey, what's wrong? Don't vanish. I need you to tell me everything you remember about that night. You must've been here with your mistress. She loved you like a child. Tell me everything you remember about anyone who came in."

He turned away from me, leapt from the bed, and seemed to place himself in the corner, as though he deserved punishment.

My heart ached for him. It was bad enough to lose someone who loved you so much, but to suffer through decades reliving whatever terrible memories he had . . . That, I couldn't imagine. "Sir Bogart, you insisted I help you solve this murder. You and Velma and Norman are the only ones I can talk to. There's not going to be any police reports or evidence lying around from an alleged suicide that took place decades ago. I know it must be awful to remember that night, but I need you to tell me everything."

Until that moment, I'd never understood the term "caterwauling." However, the sound of Sir Bogart mourning the loss of his mistress nearly broke my heart. His growly wail spilled out.

I moved toward him and made a clumsy attempt to stroke his ethereal back. "I'm sorry for asking you to remember that night. It must be horrible. I promise you'll only have to tell me once, and I'll never ask again."

Bogart turned his regal head away, too embarrassed by my presence and the depth of his emotion. He snuffled, drew a shaky breath, and told his tale. "The feline part of me had a much stronger influence when I resided on the physical plane. The interposing decades as an earthbound spirit have allowed me to expand my knowledge and understanding of the world from a different perspective. However, on that fateful night, I fear the cat was stronger than the companion."

I sat in hushed silence, waiting for the painful details to unfold.

"As you know, I had a deep and abiding admiration for chicken livers. I found one at the base of the stairs to the attic. There was a second halfway up the staircase, another at the top, and several hidden throughout the dusty boards. When I reached the top of the stairs, I heard the door close behind me." A sharp, nearly human cry pushed its way from his throat.

Making another attempt to soothe him, I stroked through his glowing energy.

He pulled away. Whether it was to punish himself or to prevent the interruption of his story, I didn't know, but he went on.

"At the time, the simple incident meant nothing. I continued to hunt for treats and eventually found my favorite cushion had been placed in the attic as well. I curled up and took what I thought was a well-deserved nap. When I awoke the following day, I scratched at the door, but none responded."

A sickening feeling swirled in my stomach. "You were trapped in the attic?"

He lifted his proud chin. "No less than I deserved. Had I resisted my basest urges, I would have been with my mistress. I could've scratched the eyes out of any who attempted to harm her."

"I'm so sorry, Bogart. When did they discover you?"

"It was several days. Norman was the only gentleman with enough honor to stand by our disgraced mistress. He searched the manor from top to bottom and eventually discovered me in the attic of Blodfyss Estate."

"I thought it was called Moonlight Manor?"

"That unceremonious edit came about nearly twenty years after she passed. A distant cousin, the last in the line, was desperate to sell the place. He felt the new name could erase the past, and would fetch a more handsome price."

"I'm sorry you didn't get to say goodbye to her."

Sir Bogart turned, arched his back sharply, and hissed.

I scooted away in terror.

"Do not offer me sympathy. I abandoned my mistress in her hour of need, and any punishment I have suffered in the afterlife will never be enough."

Swallowing shakily, I nodded. "I understand. But I'm going to need your help. You knew her better than Velma, and even Norman. You may have heard her say something or overheard a conversation that could help me solve this. I'm sorry the memories are so painful, but I need to ask about the days leading up to the party—"

He slowly lowered to his haunches and sat dejectedly. "I shall tell you all I know. The clippings in the attic may assist you. As I mentioned, you are the first to stay long enough to offer aid. The others we attempted to draw into our world fled in fear. You are our last hope, Miss Coleman."

"Let's head up to the attic. I know the clippings you're talking about, and with your help, I might be able to organize them into something that makes more sense."

The ghost of Sir Bogart vanished without a sound. Returning to the studio on the third floor, I recovered the journal. I hoped that some of her entries, combined with the clippings, would help me recreate a picture of the final days of her life.

When I reached the attic, Sir Bogart was already present.

"I apologize if this is a rude question, Bogey, but how did you die?"

"Oh, yes. My demise was self-inflicted."

"You committed suicide?" I'd never heard of such a thing.

"Indirectly. Dearest Norman took fantastic care of me for nearly seven years after that fateful night. One day, he climbed up a ladder to replace a bulb in the great chandelier and fell to his death. I was frantic. But what is a cat to do?"

A wave of sadness passed over me. This poor cat had really been through it.

"Several days passed, and I feared no one would ever come. I sought the solace of my cushion in the attic. Once again, blaming myself for the death of a beloved companion. A storm brewed, and a gust of wind closed the attic door. Several days later, a delivery arrived, and the young man discovered Norman." Bogey sighed and looked away.

"People arrived to clear the body away, and I could've cried out. I could've scratched mercilessly at the door, but I felt it was time. Time to join my mistress."

"So you died here in the attic?"

He slunk toward the cushion. "As I said, it was no less than I deserved."

Boy, this cat was breaking my heart. Moisture now welled in my eyes. "But you didn't join your mistress. You were trapped here. Why?"

"My many years as a ghost have not answered that question directly. However, I discovered my mistress was imprisoned somewhere between this world and the next. Perhaps it is a version of the purgatory people are so fond of speaking of, and perhaps I was prevented from crossing over because there was no one waiting for me. Once I entered this ghostly plane, I discovered Norman and Velma. Over time, we compared notes and expanded our powers.

Eventually, after chasing away various unworthy humans, we agreed that our purpose, our unfinished business as it were, would be to solve the mystery of our mistress's murder. Your arrival has given each of us the only hope we've felt in ages."

I swiped at the tears running down my cheeks. I'd always heard about the bond between dogs and their masters, but this sweet feline's love for Beatrix was unparalleled. "We can figure this out. I promise you."

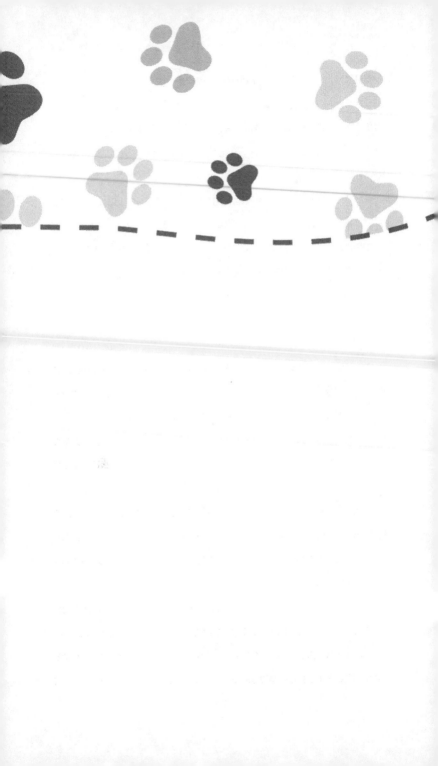

part from one quick break for the human to get some food, Sir Bogart and I spent the entire afternoon sorting through clippings, photographs, and Beatrix de Haviland's entries in her final journal. Nothing leapt out as the clue we needed to free Beatrix from her torment or Sir Bogart from his.

Once everything had been removed from the trunk, I stood to stretch my legs and work the kink out of my neck. "That's everything, Bogey. Unless you have any other information, based on the clippings, I think we can narrow it down to these three suspects." I pointed to the specific piles as I listed off the names. "Edith Plunkett, which I'm sure is no surprise to you. And then I think we need to take a closer look at this

Katherine Kelly. There were several clippings that mention her engagement to Armand. He broke the engagement off to pursue Beatrix. Maybe Katherine was upset about that."

Sir Bogart made no response. He waited silently for me to continue.

"And the last person I would put on our list is the famous starlet Marilyn Russell. She seemed pretty upset about the horrible gown they forced her to wear in that *House of Egypt* film. There were several articles, and she made some scathing remarks about Beatrix. It looks like she blames all of her lost opportunities after that on Beatrix. Whether or not that's true, I would have no way of knowing, but based on the articles, she seemed to believe it."

Bogart paced in front of the stacks and eventually nodded his majestic head. "I shall fetch the others and see what they recall of these vixens."

He returned in a flash with Velma and Norman. I went through the list of suspects, discussed my reasoning, and asked Velma if she remembered any incidents with any of the three women in the days leading up to the gala.

"Yes, Miss. That Miss Kelly came to the house, and she was quite rude to our mistress. She picked up a real expensive vase from the table in the entry and threw it at Miss de Haviland."

My eyes widened. "That sounds pretty aggressive. Does anyone remember seeing her in the ballroom during the murder? If she was that upset—"

Norman stroked his chin before shaking his head. "I believe, no, I'm sure of it, Miss Kelly was singing and playing the piano." His eyes drifted off to the distant memory. "Yes, yes. I remember now. Several people gave statements to the police, before they ruled the incident a suicide. And I myself remember hearing the delightful strains of *Swinging on a Star* down in the cellar as I selected wines for the evening. Miss Kelly was definitely not upstairs at the time of the murder."

I picked up that pile of clippings and tossed them into the trunk. "That leaves us with the angry starlet and the rival costumer. Anyone remember seeing Marilyn Russell in the ballroom?"

Silence.

"Wow. Maybe it was her?" I couldn't believe it was that easy.

Velma pressed a hand to her mouth and shook her head. "No, I remember something coming to the house—from a messenger. It were the day before the incident with Miss Kelly. A messenger came with a large box, and I took it up to our mistress."

Nodding with interest, I gestured for her to continue. "What was in the box?"

She shook her head and looked at the floor. "It were that terrible dress. Miss Russell had slashed it to ribbons and threatened to do the same to Miss de Haviland if she ever tried to design another gown for Miss Russell."

I pressed a hand to my forehead. "Good gracious. Beatrix really knew how to make enemies."

Norman cleared his throat. "She was a passionate and creative woman. However, I remember receiving a letter from Miss Russell, saying that under no circumstances would she ever attend a gala at the home of someone so beneath her. The exact words escape me, but Miss Russell was not in attendance. She was never admitted to the manor."

Picking up that stack of clippings, I tossed them into the trunk and shrugged. "Well, then it had to be Edith Plunkett. Unless one of you can think of another fight or threat?"

The three ghosts exchanged confused looks, and I waited for their agreement with my conclusion. Yet it never came.

"What's wrong? What makes you think it wasn't Edith Plunkett?"

Norman sighed. "Miss Plunkett was not well. Knowing what I know now, it must've been the first month's sickness that some women experience with pregnancy, madam. At the time, she claimed an upset stomach, and I had taken her to the drawing room and offered her a glass of water. She was quite unsteady on her feet when she accepted the water. I can't imagine her having the strength to commit such a crime."

Velma glowed like a giant candelabra. "Wait. Sir Armand."

"What about him?" My breath caught, and I glanced between them, certain the extra luminesce meant she'd thought of something important. Could it be *the* clue?

"He came into the kitchen when I were preparing the tea tray. He had a glass in one hand, and when I asked if he needed something, he shouted at me to mind my station, and said he were retrieving a glass of water for his fiancé."

Norman's eyes brightened as though he'd suspected the duplicitous man for a long time. "But I'd already taken water to her. He must've been mixing up the poison at that time."

I clapped my hands to get the apparitions' attention. When they all turned toward me, I spoke. "But we know Beatrix never drank that poison in the little bottle. No lipstick, remember? So that doesn't explain how the poison got into her system."

The energy in the room faded as though someone had pushed an off switch. Their expressions drooped, and Norman's brightness faded.

Velma bobbed her head innocently and looked toward me. "But maybe it were him that killed me. For seeing the glass. For maybe having the clue we needed to lay the murder at his feet. If he was taking water to his fiancé, then perhaps the poison was within the glass."

I nodded slowly. "Which room did you take them to, Norman?"

He straightened his vest and tilted his head. "Yes, I'd forgotten he was with her. I left Armand and his fiancé both in the drawing room. So he knew his fiancé already had the water. After I left them to themselves, I immediately went to the cellar and returned to check on them after opening the wine for supper."

I jumped with excitement. "Did Armand know about the secret passage?"

Norman's face seemed to darken with guilt, but he

didn't answer. His expression hardened as though he expected to be badgered for what he might consider gossip.

My heart twisted. "Norman, we're all on the same team. Tell me what you know. You might have the information we need to solve this."

He glanced at Sir Bogart and Velma. "I apologize, my dear friends. Miss de Haviland was in the habit of having me guide late-night guests into the drawing room and leave them unattended. She would—I do apologize for the impropriety of it." He cleared his throat, the sound thinner coming from his ghostly self. "She would come down through the secret passage from the burgundy room, and escort guests upstairs."

That was as close as Norman would come to impugning his former mistress's decency.

I stared beyond my trio of specter witnesses, still puzzling on the unsolved mystery of Moonlight Manor. "We know she and Armand had been romantically involved, so he would have knowledge of the secret passage. Maybe Edith was in on it. Maybe she pretended to be ill so that you would take them to the drawing room. Then Armand snuck through that secret passage and killed Beatrix."

The butler shook his head. "Begging your pardon,

madam. But I saw Miss de Haviland before the authorities took her away. She had no marks on her. I fail to see how he—" Norman couldn't finish the sentence.

Frowning, I turned. "No empty glasses were found anywhere and certainly none with her lipstick on them. Is that correct?"

All nodded their agreement. Sir Bogart also flicked his tail.

"Velma, you said you saw your mistress ready to make a grand entrance when Armand and Edith entered. What was she wearing at the time you last saw her?"

Velma scratched her gray-blond curls and tucked a loose strand of hair under her head covering. "Well, Miss. It were a gorgeous emerald green dress that she worked on for months. She had that fabric brought in from France, and the lace had been handmade just for the gown. In fact, it were so beautiful she wouldn't even wear her jewels. Said it were her finest work, she did."

This time, I directed my question toward the loyal butler. "All right. And what was she wearing when you saw them take the body away, Norman?"

Norman glanced from Velma to me, and back again. "She was wearing the same gown, but—" His image suddenly flickered with potent emotion, and he struggled to maintain corporeal form. "It's here. I'm certain of it."

Sir Bogart leapt to the top of an old hall tree, his fur standing on end from excitement. "Yes, I recall seeing it. Norman retrieved the gown from the hospital, and I believe it ended up in this attic."

My jaw slackened. "If it's here, perhaps it holds the clue we need to be able to put this all to rest."

The three ghosts searched feverishly, and I joined them as they passed through item after item in their haste to find the missing garment.

Finally, in the far corner of the attic, Norman called out. "Here." He was too excited to pick it up, unable to keep focus long enough to do so. "It's here."

Paper rustled as he lifted a box from behind a piece of furniture while the lid hid the crafted beauty inside. I hurried toward the gown Norman held and as I reached for it, a strange warning sprang to life in my head. *Don't touch the pin.*

I paused before grasping the box. Who had warned me? Had it been Beatrix? It hadn't been an audible instruction, but it had been a warning all the same. Norman removed the lid, and I carefully reached for the dress and brought it toward the light. It was exactly as Velma had described.

Gorgeous by any standards, even though age had dulled its shine.

Velma pointed to a corsage, fastened to the front of the bodice. "That weren't on there when I saw the mistress."

Sir Bogart leapt down from the hat rack and loped close, crunching his nose. "It doesn't look fine enough for my lady."

The sight of the corsage took me back. I went to my high school prom alone. After I got myself a corsage, I unceremoniously pinned it on my hand-me-down dress. I thought I could show everyone up by being brave enough to attend without a date. Turned out that pricking myself when I pinned on my cheap carnation was only the beginning of the pain I'd suffer that evening. My eyebrows lowered, and I shuddered.

"What is it, mistress?" Sir Bogey lifted one paw eagerly and called me back from the dark memory that nearly engulfed me.

Clearing my mind, I carefully opened the dress across a small wooden stool, lifting it out of the box and turning it this way and that.

"See anything?" Velma asked.

"Do you see this?" I pointed to a small brown stain on the inside of the dress—directly under the corsage. It could have been tea or some other liquid, but a part of me knew it wasn't. I suspected it had to be blood. Maybe this was what we'd come to find.

Velma leaned forward. "I had nowhere near the skills of Miss de Haviland, but even I ain't likely to poke myself like that."

Norman nodded vigorously and pointed to the corsage. "They're dried and wrinkled, madam, but I'd know them anywhere. Those are mock orange blossoms. Four rounded petals, rather than five pointed. The mock orange flower means deceit."

"So Armand snuck up the secret passage, told her some terrible lie, and stabbed her with a poison pin on a corsage." I shook my head in disgust. "What else could it be?"

Sir Bogart snarled. "He had already dealt the deadly blow when Velma witnessed him in the kitchen. The entire scene with the suicide note was a fabrication—a hoax."

Velma sobbed. "What a horrible man."

Nodding, I added my two cents. "Let's not forget about Edith. She must've known what he was doing. Maybe she even blackmailed him with threats of revealing the illegitimate child? I'm sure she didn't trust him to be faithful—after what he'd done with her while in another relationship."

20

The heavens didn't open, and there was no triumphant cheer. Listening intently, I gazed at the shimmering faces of the three ghosts gathered in the attic and shook my head. "There should be a noise or a feeling. We solved it, right? Shouldn't you all disappear or something?"

They exchanged glances, and it was clear they had no more information than me.

I crouched beside the transparent feline on the floor. "Bogey, you were closest to your mistress. Can you communicate with her or somehow sense if she's crossed over?"

The regal cat lifted his whiskered chin and closed his glowing eyes while we all waited in silence.

Before his eyes popped open, the now familiar swirling black void opened behind him.

Beatrix de Haviland appeared, much as she had before. Her raven hair had been piled in beautiful curls atop her head, and, in the vision, the glimmering green dress still possessed its original glory. Her long fingers reached toward the mock orange flower on the bodice. In the vision, the blooms were still fresh, and I swallowed sharply.

She stretched her left hand toward me, and I strained with every part of my body. Squinting at her mouth, I tried to make it all out. Her lips moved, but I couldn't understand what she was saying. Still, she reached for me.

Turning toward Norman and Velma, I asked, "Can either of you make out what she's saying?"

Velma arched an eyebrow, but she didn't answer me. Norman's mouth hung slack.

Trembling, I pointed toward the swirling void behind Bogey. "Can't you see her? It's Beatrix. She's right there. She has a message, and I can't understand what she's trying to say."

Norman clutched at his heart, and Velma whimpered.

"Sir Bogart, can't they see her?" I rasped.

He shook his head slowly, and the sharp angles of

his powerful jaw shifted in the light. "They cannot. I can no more explain that mystery than I can explain the ruthless actions of Edith and Armand. Look deeply into her eyes, Miss Coleman. She could disappear at any moment."

My throat dried, and I shuddered. It was up to me and Bogey to understand what the murdered mistress of the manor was trying to convey. "Do you understand what she's saying?"

He sighed. "No, I cannot. It is up to you, Miss Coleman."

Swallowing back the fear quaking through my body, I stepped toward the void and locked eyes with the specter of Beatrix de Haviland.

Several times in a row, her bright red lips moved in the same pattern. She repeated one word over and over. Scowling, my gaze didn't leave her. What word?

I struggled to make out the word she so carefully formed with her perfect lips. "Roof?" I echoed. "Is it roof?"

She shook her head, and her mouth moved again.

"Move?" Fiddlesticks. The task was up to me, and I was badly botching it. What was she trying to express?

She shook her head and tapped the flower pinned to her dress.

"Proof," I announced, suddenly certain it was what she was trying to say. As soon as the word left my lips, the void closed with a snap, and all ghostly eyes turned toward me.

Velma's hand fluttered at her throat, and Norman's lips formed a tight line.

Sir Bogart settled on his back haunches. "Please elaborate, Miss Coleman."

"The only thing I can guess is that she can't cross-over until we have actual proof. We have to clear her name." I frowned. "We looked through everything, and we have a great theory, but I guess it's not enough to free her spirit. There's no way we can get proof. Not anymore." Looking at the sad faces of the ghostly trio, I collapsed to the floor of the attic.

"Theatrics, Miss Coleman?"

I glared at Sir Bogart. "What happens to my Bed-and-Breakfast if I can't help Beatrix move on?"

Velma and Norman didn't respond; in fact, they kept their eyes on the floors.

But Sir Bogart trotted around me and back to the spot he'd been before. "What do we do next, Miss Coleman?"

"Give up?"

"We have no choice but to move ahead. You are the only soul who has tried to solve the murder, and you are the only one who can help us. You must not give up, Miss Coleman. Moving ahead is now the only way to save your livelihood."

I sighed and climbed back to my feet. The cat had a point. What could we have missed and what could we do now?

"What do we do now?" Norman asked. "What proof can we find?"

I lifted the dress once more and gazed at the pin poking through the glamorous fabric. "What we need is some kind of lab to test the pin. I'm sure they could find traces of the poison. But I don't know how to run those kinds of tests, and it's not like I can call up Sheriff Allen and tell her I have to solve a mystery for a ghost."

Sir Bogart's expression changed in an instant. He strutted toward me, and his proud demeanor had returned.

I blinked as I considered the apparent change in his mood. "Well, don't you look like a sly fox?"

His back arched, and he hissed vehemently. "I should prefer if you never compare me to a canine."

Inclining my head, I conceded. "My apologies, Sir Bogart. Perhaps I should've said you looked like the cat that swallowed the canary."

He snickered, and his whiskers bounced up and

down. "Now that I have done. But it has nothing to do with my current mood."

"Then what are you smiling about?"

Sir Bogart certainly seemed pleased with himself. He sauntered around me then took a seat. "You have unwittingly given us the solution we require. You must call Sheriff Allen at once."

I rubbed my tired eyes and shook my head. "You misunderstood, Bogey. I said I *couldn't* do that. Sheriff Allen isn't going to make a trip out to the manor to pick up a dead flower and a straight pin." My shoulders drooped, and I sighed loudly.

Bogey curled his tail around his feet and tilted his head in a quite superior manner. "She will if you tell her it is a favor for Sir Bogart."

My head popped up. "What? There's absolutely no way Sheriff Allen knows you. Sorry to remind you, but you died decades before she was born."

He lifted a single claw and scraped it along the side of one of his gleaming incisors. "True. However, Haley was an adventurous child. She found a window with a broken lock at the back of the manor. She visited me often in her youth."

I raised a hand, processing what Sir Bogart implied. "Hold on, you told me only the owner of the manor could see you and talk to you."

Bogey wagged his head back and forth, and his whiskers twitched. "Her bravery knew no bounds. One evening, she scampered through the rear window with her bedroll and crept up to the attic. She lit a candle and called out to the spirits of the manor. And then she announced, 'I, Haley Allen, am the mistress of Moonlight Manor.' " Bogey chuckled. "At which point, I appeared and welcomed her, nearly sending her tumbling down the stairs."

My eyes were as wide as saucers. "What happened next?"

He peered at the attic's exit as though recalling the meeting. "She screamed and raced downstairs. However, I beat her to her escape window and somehow convinced her to stay. She visited often, and then one day—" His eyes filled with sadness and he couldn't finish his story.

My heart twisted for the lonely feline. "I suppose one day she got too old for ghost stories and she never came back. I'm sorry, Bogey."

He attempted to shrug his shoulders, but I could see the loss of the only friend he'd had in years still caused him pain. He'd probably borne the consequences of Beatrix de Haviland's death more than anyone. If nothing else, I was committed to give Beatrix her peace for Sir Bogart's sake. Calling Sheriff

Allen might be a long shot, but it was the one shot we had.

Taking all three of my ghostly acquaintances in, I nodded once. "Okay, team. I'm going to call the sheriff. If they come and arrest me, or lock me up in an asylum, I blame you three."

Norman's face grew stern. "We will never let that happen, madam. You are the mistress of the manor now, and we will use all the powers of this world and the next to keep you from harm."

His brave words touched my heart, and I drew my cell phone from its usual place in my pocket. My hands shook as I dialed the number. Putting the call on speaker, I placed it on a shelf beside us and crossed my fingers.

When Sheriff Allen came on the line, I thought I might lose my nerve. Bogey nudged me with his head, and Norman attempted to pat my shoulder. They weren't about to let me back down, so I tried to keep my request as vague as possible.

"This is Sheriff Allen," she repeated.

Clearing my throat, I forged ahead. "Sorry to bother you, Sheriff. There's been another incident at Moonlight Manor. There's some evidence I need you to run through your lab."

Then she informed me that local law enforcement

managed investigations, and items would be sent to the crime lab at her discretion. She paused to wait for my response.

I swallowed loudly, took a deep breath, and prepared to utter the phrase that could land me in the psych ward. "Sheriff Allen, I was told to tell you it's a personal favor for Sir Bogart."

There was nothing but total silence on the other end of the line. After twenty seconds, I wasn't sure if she'd hung up. I grabbed the phone off the shelf to check for a dropped call. No, it was still connected.

"Sheriff? Sheriff Allen, are you still there?"

Her strong, confident voice had lowered to little more than a whisper. "I'm on my way."

I ended the call and tucked the phone into my pocket. Still in the attic, the four of us rejoiced like spring fairies in a moonlit meadow. When our celebration concluded, I carefully collected the dress and met my ghostly companions in the first-floor foyer as we anxiously awaited Haley's—Sheriff Allen's—arrival.

When the tires crunched along the gravel, my heart stuttered. I really wanted this to work, and it was within our grasp. Beatrix de Haviland required proof enough to correct her cause of death and clear her name.

Opening the door before Sheriff Allen could knock, I welcomed her into the drawing room. "Can I get you some water or a pop?"

She shook her head, and her eyes scanned the room. "Is he here right now?"

I gestured toward the ottoman where Sir Bogart reclined. "Yes, there. Lounging. Do you want me to tell you the whole story from start to finish?"

She stared at the round, overstuffed footstool, and it was clear she could no longer see the feline's apparition. Suddenly, her intelligent blue eyes searched my face. "So I wasn't just a lonely kid imagining things?"

I shook my head. "No, Haley. You weren't."

"I'll take that drink now," she murmured.

After fetching a glass of water, I told Sheriff Allen the story of the murder of Beatrix de Haviland. I laid out all the evidence, listed the suspects we'd reviewed in our investigation, and shared the final theory that had made the most sense. Finally, taking a deep breath, I pointed toward the round table in the grand entry. "That's the dress Beatrix was wearing when she was murdered. If we're right about this, there should be traces of arsenic on the pin, and that stain on the inside of the dress would be blood."

Sheriff Allen shrugged her shoulders and exhaled

a long, slow breath. "And if you're right, if there is poison on that pin, then Beatrix will be free?"

"That's what I'm hoping. I think it has to be an official decision. Somehow you have to announce that new evidence came to light in the suicide of Beatrix de Haviland, and that it has been reclassified as a homicide. It's the whole suicide accusation that's trapping her in between. As far as I can tell." I threw my hands up and shook my head. "I know how crazy this all sounds."

Sheriff Haley Allen lumbered to her feet, walked silently to the foyer, and reverently collected the dress. She moved with purpose but also somehow appeared as if she'd aged in the time since she'd arrived. Maybe she'd realized she'd left Sir Bogart alone all those years.

"Are you all right, sheriff?"

"I'm fine." She took a deep breath and let it out slowly. "I'll get this to the lab right away. If there's arsenic on that pin, I'll come up with something." She gazed longingly at the ottoman and smiled. "I won't let you down, Sir Bogart. I owe you that much."

The way she spoke to the ghostly cat warmed my heart, and I escorted her out of Moonlight Manor with a warm smile. Carefully, I closed the door behind her and sagged against it.

The wait began now.

* * *

Each hour that passed after Sheriff Allen left Moonlight Manor seemed like a day. The four of us were tense, nervous, anxious, eager, and hesitantly excited. We paced through the manor and clustered together. Each time my cell phone rang, we expected Sheriff Allen to be on the other end to deliver life-changing news. We paced through the manor.

That afternoon, even the big news of the sale of our wine bringing in just over $18,000 could barely distract us from our fixation with the hands on the grandfather clock. I listened to the instructions from the auction house representative with only half my mind. How long did it take to test for poison?

Nearing sunset, when my cell phone finally rang with the awaited call, I felt as though I left my body for a moment as I tapped speaker. "Sheriff Allen? Do you have news for us?"

The sheriff wasted no time. "You were right. Positive for arsenic. And it was blood on the dress. I met with the president of the historical society, and he's agreed to release a statement to the press in exchange for the dress, pin, and corsage. We didn't get into the details, but there will be an official article in the paper, and on the historical society's website, revealing the new details that came to light in the infamous Beatrix de Haviland case. Her suicide will officially be reclassified as a homicide."

I smiled then. "That's great news."

"You did well," Sheriff Allen added.

Norman and Velma hugged. Sir Bogart raced up the imperial staircase, around the second floor, and back down. His immense joy could not be contained, and I beamed at them all.

Finally, I thanked the sheriff profusely, ended the call, and stared at my ghostly compatriots. They would now be leaving soon, wouldn't they? I wasn't sure how I felt about the idea of being alone in the manor. But I wasn't about to tell any of them that. They had to move on, get on with their existence in the new plane. Would Beatrix de Haviland appear to express her gratitude in person?

Instead, an inexplicable rumble rolled through the manor, and an other-worldly smell I couldn't place scented the air. A light fog moved over the ground, and I believed Beatrix discovered she was free to move on. Sir Bogart, Velma, and Norman all shared a long look. The light in the manor turned warm, and I wasn't sure if it was from the sunset or the news.

Beatrix did not appear, but far away laughter echoed through the manor. Something broke free in my heart, and radiant delight took its place. As the light faded, I braced for the others to disappear as well, but they remained with me in the foyer.

Silently, I studied them as they considered me. Finally, I gestured to them. "You're all still here? If her death was your unfinished business, shouldn't you be leaving?"

Sir Bogart the Eternal tilted his wise head and gazed up at the butler and the cook. Something unspoken passed between them, and I pressed a hand to my chest. "What is it? What's happening?"

Bogey leapt onto the round table and fixed me with an unreadable stare. "My former mistress has indeed been released. We all felt it. However, we've chosen to stay. Here." He blinked. "With you, Miss Coleman."

All the tears I'd been holding back since Lucas Aconite dumped me came flooding through. "But why? Why would you choose to stay?"

Bogey attempted to look aloof, but there was a depth of gratitude in his eyes that could not be ignored. "We make a good match, the four of us.

We've decided to stay and help you run this accommodation and meals operation you spoke of."

His formal description of a B&B gripped me with laughter and I swept away the tears. They hadn't wanted to leave me alone in the manor, and I hadn't wanted them to go. Not really.

I offered a sad smile. "Oh, it's too late, Bogey. I'm afraid that ship has sailed. We'll be able to keep the lights on for a few weeks with the money from the sale of the rare wines, but after that—"

Norman clasped his hands together and leaned forward. "We simply need a second plan, madam."

"Yes," I agreed. "We need what's called a Plan B. And I'm fresh out."

Velma tucked a curl behind her ear and bobbed her head. "Is it the ghosts, miss?"

"Oh, I'm not blaming anyone. But Mr. Griffin's article did mention strange paranormal happenings, and he made them sound negative and terrifying, not entertaining."

She continued to bob her head. "That's just it, miss. What if it were entertaining?"

Norman's face split in a grin.

I tilted my head. "What do you mean?"

"Well, I ain't that good at keeping track of time,

but it seems it's getting close to Mischief Night. What if we all chipped in to cause extra mischief?"

My eyes widened. "I don't follow."

A glow engulfed Sir Bogart, and he grinned wickedly. "I believe our fair Velma is on to something intriguing, mistress. Rather than attempt to hide your ghosts, put them on display for all to see. This could be the finest haunted mansion on the eastern seaboard. Surely a great many would pay to experience the spectacle."

At first, I didn't answer. Was I seriously considering this? It seemed crazy, but then again…

Sir Bogart raised a ghostly paw. "Do you call the night in question Halloween?"

I could hardly breathe. "It's brilliant. An authentic haunted mansion. Just in time for All Hallows Eve." I jumped up and down, and would not be embarrassed to admit I squealed. It had to work. Many ghost hunters and thrill-seekers were interested in the paranormal, weren't they? "Velma, you're a genius. Let's get to work on this immediately. Moonlight Manor is going to be the can't-miss venue of the season."

Sir Bogart took a well-deserved bow, and the four of us moved our team meeting to the sturdy kitchen table. I took notes, while my ghostly conspirators revealed decade's worth of their most mischievous tricks. Once a few well-placed social media posts got the ball rolling, reservations would begin rolling in.

It was going to be a Happy Halloween, after all.

An ancient grimoire. A family curse. Will Halloween bring treats or death for Sydney this year?

CLICK HERE to get your copy of *Moonlight and Magic,* so that you can keep reading this series today!

WHAT'S NEXT?

Sydney Coleman is coexisting with her ghostly roommates. But if she hopes to keep the Gothic manor, she has to bring in some cash. Charging for haunted Halloween tours could save them, if it doesn't kill her first...

It's a pity she didn't listen when the lordly feline warned her not to toy with the spellbook. Now Sydney's reliving the same day over and over—and every loop ends with a corpse on the floor and her in handcuffs.

Can Sydney unravel the confusing clues, or will time run out?

What happens next?
Don't wait to find out…

MOONLIGHT AND MAGIC is now available.

Purchase your copy so that you can keep reading
this zany mystery series today!

SNEAK PEEK

MOONLIGHT & MAGIC

Operations were underway for the most buzz-worthy thing to happen at Moonlight Manor since the murder of Beatrix de Haviland. The Gothic mansion and its three resident ghosts, including the self-appointed feline Lord of the Manor, Sir Bogart, were finally going to capitalize on history.

Trust me when I tell you, they took blessed little convincing, and now I couldn't be more thrilled to serve as mistress to the haunted manor. Banging echoed out front, and I wasn't sure if it was repairs or ghosts. My grand opening was shaping up to be quite the event.

My escape from New York City to the sleepy town in Maine called Misty Meadows had been bumpy at best. But my luck was about to change. There could be no better use for a massive nineteenth-century mansion, rumored to be haunted, than a series of ghostly tours during the spookiest season of the year. All Hallows Eve would never be the same.

Sure, the guests would assume that everything had been done with the proverbial 'smoke and mirrors,' but my trio of ghosts and I would know the truth. The haunting of Moonlight Manor was as real as could be.

It was incredibly fortunate that freckle-faced baker Frannie Clark and I had hit it off before I'd even officially moved to town. She, too, had migrated from the Midwest to the East Coast and done a soul-sucking stint in New York City. Frannie understood me. And more importantly, she didn't force me to give her details I preferred to keep private. She accepted me and supported me, especially when it came to the phantom friends in residence at Moon-light Manor.

Plus, one thing Frannie was absolutely unstop-pable at was gathering the troops. She knew everyone in town, knew what they were good at, and knew how to get ahold of them. She'd found someone to help me clean the manor when I moved in, she'd found someone to lend me a car, and best of all, she'd convinced Davis Martin, the ox-shouldered son of the local hardware store owner, to serve as my handyman in exchange for free pastries from her bakery. I tried to offer him money on more than one occasion, but his crooked-grin answer was always the same.

"Keep your money," he said. "Frannie's got me covered."

Yet I'd seen the man eat. How Frannie made enough for him, I didn't understand. I couldn't imagine how she planned to keep Heaven Can Bake afloat with this guy running a tab, but I was extremely grateful for the help, and it was my handyman whose help I needed right now.

"Davis?" I called.

"Out front."

When I caught sight of him, I had to stop on the broad stone terrace in front of the manor and lean against the wrought-iron railing to catch my breath. One would think that the fall weather in Maine would require more clothing than carpenter pants and a skin tight T-shirt drenched with sweat. As I stared at the thirst-trap of a man in my yard, I could barely force myself to swallow. Having this guy around meant I required repeated reminders—I'd sworn off men. After the selfish ex I left behind in New York, I didn't need the mess in my newly restarted life.

I sighed and tipped my head as I watched Davis wrap an extension cord around his arm. What would it be like to be that lucky, little extension cord?

Davis dropped the coiled cord in his hand and shaded his eyes against the bright sun. "Whaddya need, Syd?"

Blinking, I brought my brain back to the reason I needed to hunt him down. "Um . . . Updates."

He nodded once and picked up a collection of shims. "One sec."

It made me happy to know that things between us had become more casual. At least some of the time. When we first met, he tried to call me Miss Coleman every time, and when I insisted on Sydney, he simply switched to Miss Sydney. However, the old manor home was feeling a lot like owning a boat, which meant there was always something to fix. So Davis and I had fallen into a comfortable rhythm.

He placed the smaller pieces of wood in a neat pile to the side, dropped a handful of wire ends into a bin, and then straightened. "Which updates did you want?"

I stepped toward him, barely able to contain my excitement. "How's it going with the lights? I can absolutely picture what you're saying about the up-lighting making the towers look spooky and mysterious, but I can't wait to see it."

He grinned, and his green eyes held a hint of pride. "Yeah, it'll be great. Did you ever tell spooky stories around the campfire when you were a kid?"

I nodded, but I didn't understand where he was going with his question. Perhaps I was too distracted by his nearness. Yes, that was definitely it.

"Did you ever hold a flashlight under your chin? Changes your whole face. You're gonna freak out when you see what the manor looks like by the end." He picked up the heavy loops of electrical cable and got back to work on the repairs under the porch eaves.

Walking down the granite steps to the circle encompassing the fountain in the front yard, I turned and gazed up at my mansion.

My mansion. Yes, I was getting used to saying it, but I still didn't completely believe it. How had I wound up with a mansion? With towers. *With towers!* I mentally squealed. One day I was grinding it out at a thankless ad agency job, with a secretly sleazy ex, and the next I was living in a haunted mansion.

Life sure had a strange way of guiding us into new adventures. A failure in New York had brought me to

Misty Meadows. It still boggled my mind now and then.

A strange tingle spread across my scalp, interrupting my wool-gathering, and I felt compelled to turn back toward the fountain. I laid my hand on the low wall circling the unused water feature.

"Hey, do you know if this thing runs?" I called over my shoulder before turning around.

Davis scraped the sandy-brown hair back from his sweaty forehead and grinned as he jogged down the steps to join me. "Only one way to find out."

I stepped back and gave him room to work.

He popped open a flat stone access panel and peered inside.

"See anything?"

"No immediate snakes or spiders."

I shuddered. "I should hope not. It's getting a little cold out this season for snakes."

He gave me a squinty-eyed wink and got right to it. There were wrenches, screwdrivers, and at one point even a crowbar, but eventually a trickle of water dripped from the vase that was held by a lady.

I peered up at the statue as the water dribbled over it. "It's sort of working. There's a little water coming out of her pot."

Davis straightened and gazed at me in mock

horror. "Did you just call the eternal vessel of love, held in the arms of the incredibly beautiful goddess Aphrodite, a pot?"

My eyes widened, and I shook my head. "No. Of course not."

His warm laughter softened the blow of my lack of knowledge. "Don't worry. I didn't know either. I overheard Augusta Adams tearing into somebody at the hardware store. Don't ask me how they landed on the topic of an old fountain at Moonlight Manor, but they said something about Diana and a water pitcher, and old Augusta let 'em have it." Then he disappeared into the inner-working of the water feature once more.

I chuckled, but not as easily as Davis. Augusta was something else.

Finally, he gave a triumphant snort. "Ah ha, here it is, you only thought you could hide your inner workings from me . . ." Davis muttered. Then his voice trailed away as my thoughts turned to the others I'd met during my adventure in business-owning.

I'd been warned more than once about Augusta's temper. That woman had an unmatched reputation in town for architectural and historical expertise, and she did not suffer fools on either topic. Plus, she was the founder and sole owner of the Adams School of Colonial Arts. Her fine work had repaired a damaged pane of antique stained glass at the mansion, after someone hurled a rock through. In addition to the repair, she paid the hooligan, Gladys Williams, a personal visit after the incident. Yikes.

If only that had been the last time I'd had a run in with busybody and amateur vandal Gladys Williams. However, since the start of publicizing the haunted mansion tours, I could count on near daily visits from my angry neighbor. How she had so much time on her hands with her own manor, I didn't understand. She had to have staff taking care of things, if she could afford to always be causing problems in my business ventures.

Though, she never had a direct complaint. It was always more of a random threat about a vague violation. If she could be believed, she had the entire book of city codes memorized, and *my* manor was breaking most of them.

It got so bad this past week, I had to call Sheriff Haley Allen out and have the woman officially escorted off my property. Sheriff Allen had been as grim-faced about the ordeal as I'd ever seen her.

Which, in case you're not familiar, meant that the sheriff told the violator that they were never to set foot on the property again, and if they did, they would be arrested and officially charged with trespassing. The way the sheriff explained it to me, was that it was similar to a restraining order, but without getting the courts involved.

Gladys seemed harmless enough, so it sounded like the type of deterrent that would be effective. I hoped the warning worked in a long-term way. Gladys didn't need to have anything to do with my grand opening.

Correction: She didn't need to have any opportunity to foul up my grand opening.

At my feet, Davis grunted. "Oof. Found a spider."

"Are you okay?"

"Fine. Fine. Ah, there's the problem." He didn't add anything else.

Another splatter came out of the pot, and I turned to watch the liquid slip down the statue. Davis kept banging.

Additional clanging, screeching, and a strange gurgling thump were followed by a massive spout of water—which caught me square in the face.

Screaming, I jumped back. I scrubbed at my face, already trying to calculate how old the liquid was. How long had it been there inside the fountain? Did it matter?

Davis scrambled out from whatever secret interior fountain panel he'd been working on and covered his mouth. Not necessarily in surprise. It was more to hide his laughter.

"Davis. I'm soaked." I immediately started to shiver in the cool air of autumn.

He jogged to my side of the fountain, scooped an arm around me, and hurried me indoors, into the foyer. "You're freezing. Let's get you into some dry clothes, Miss Coleman."

Through chattering teeth, I admonished him. "For the—the—umpteenth time, Davis, c-c-call me Sydney. You know how much I hate Miss Coleman. And the water is not your fault. I was the one st-st-anding right in front of Aphrodite's b-b-bottomless jug of love or whatever you called it." My whole body quaked with cold. "How long do you think that water was in there? Do you think I need a dose of antibiotics or something?"

He laughed and shook his head. "Oh, no, no antibiotics necessary, Sydney. Water was from further inside the statue than all that. Now you get upstairs and dry off. We can't have you catch your death of a cold right before your grand opening."

I wrapped my arms around myself and vigorously rubbed the goosebumps on my arms. "Th-th-thanks.

Let me know when you get the fountain under control."

He bounded out the front door, still chuckling, and called over his shoulder, "Will do."

Sir Bogart, my feline overlord, appeared next to me on the steps. His silky black fur glowed to perfection and his intelligent yellow eyes sparked with secrets. "I feel quite certain that young man is sweet on you, mistress."

My grimace didn't seem to deter Sir Bogart. So I added, "Not today, Sir Matchmaker. As you know, I have bigger fish to fry."

He shrugged his lithe shoulders and vanished, mumbling something about fish.

I hurried to my bedroom, the blue room, on the second floor, slipped into dry clothes, and twisted my wet hair out of the way. At least the fountain mishap was mechanical and not paranormal. Davis could finish fixing that up with no problem. But if I was going to make any progress on my final checklist, I needed to get up to the attic and mine for more treasures. I'd set a $150 budget for decorations, and if I had any chance of sticking to the budget, the rest of the dusty décor would have to be found on-site and repurposed.

I scanned my second-floor room, checking for

something large enough to carry items back down out of the attic above the third floor. My laundry hamper looked about the right size to carry a load of fantastic finds. I dumped my dirty clothes onto the floor—to be honest, most of them were already there, paused en route to the washing—and headed toward the third level and the only other robin's-egg-blue glass handle that had called to me on my first visit to the manor.

The little door to the attic had the same gorgeous blue glass knob my bedroom had. Cobalt glass must be the way to my heart, and I imagined where else I could tuck cobalt accents on the second and third floors. Someday.

Yet a mere foot from the narrow door leading to my attic, a disconcerting interruption derailed my decorating plans. I frowned at the angry sounds coming from outside the manor.

Now what? At this rate, I'd never complete the finishing touches on the manor.

MOONLIGHT AND MAGIC is now available.

Purchase your copy so that you can keep reading this zany mystery series today!

ABOUT TRIXIE SILVERTALE

Trixie Silvertale grew up reading an endless supply of Lilian Jackson Braun, Hardy Boys, and Nancy Drew novels. She loves the amateur sleuths in cozy mysteries and obsesses about all things paranormal. Those two passions unite in her paranormal cozy mystery series, and she's thrilled to write them and share them with you.

When she's not consumed by writing, she bakes to fuel her creative engine and pulls weeds in her herb garden to clear her head (*and sometimes she pulls out her hair, but mostly weeds*).

If you're looking for more from Trixie Silvertale, sign up for her monthly newsletter at **trixiesilver tale.com/paranormal-cozy-club-2/**

Greetings are welcome:
trixie@trixiesilvertale.com
Bookbub | Facebook | Instagram

Click here to **Join Trixie's Club!**

A NOTE FROM TRIXIE

I've always been a huge fan of haunted mansions . . .

The best part of "living" in Misty Meadows was the chance to build a brand new world, and meet Sydney Coleman and Sir Bogart. And big "spooky" hugs to the world's best ARC Team – Trixie's Mystery ARC Detectives!

It was an honor and a pleasure to work with Molly Fitz and Whiskered Mysteries. They offered me the opportunity to step into a wonderful new tale for a book or three, and I loved it.

I'm especially grateful for the helpful architecture info provided by Michael. Thanks to Josh and Morgan for making me watch scary movies!

FUN FACT: When I was in high school, I toured a haunted mansion. During the tour, I snuck away from the group, climbed over a velvet rope, and explored an off-limits area! I didn't see a ghost, but it was quite a thrill.

SECRET: I'm a massive fan of costume design, and have a minor in technical theater.

I hope you'll continue to explore the mansion with us.

TRIXIE SILVERTALE (SEPTEMBER 2022)

MITZY MOON MYSTERIES

A gift that's too good to be true. A murder she didn't commit. A barista in a latte trouble...

Mitzy Moon believes she's an orphan, so she's dumbstruck when a special delivery to her low-rent apartment reveals a family. But her shock turns to awe when she discovers her grandmother left her a fortune, a fiendish feline, and a bookshop of rare tomes brimming with magic. Start with Book 1: **Fries and Alibis**.

MAGICAL RENAISSANCE FAIRE MYSTERIES

A dubious festival. A fatal swim. Can this fortune-telling fairy herald the true killer?

Coriander the Conjurer is trapped in a cursed Renaissance Faire, but that's the good news. Her usual routine of reading patrons' futures and compensating for her lopsided fairy wings is interrupted when a scuffle turns deadly. Now, in order to broker peace within the realm she must solve a mermaid's murder. But she'll need the help of a dangerous vampire and her meddling toad familiar to uncover the real clues. Start the adventure with **All Swell That Ends Spell.**

MORE MOLLY

ABOUT MOLLY FITZ

While USA Today bestselling author Molly Fitz can't technically talk to animals, she and her three feline writing assistants have deep and very animated conversations as they navigate their days.

She lives with her comedian husband, diva daughter, and their own private zoo somewhere in the wilds of Alaska. Molly will occasionally venture out for good food, great coffee, or to meet new animal friends.

Learn more about Molly and her books, and be sure to sign up for her newsletter at:
    www.MollyMysteries.com

ALSO BY MOLLY FITZ

Learn more about Molly's collected works, so that you can decide which book you'd like to read next...

PET WHISPERER P.I.

Angie Russo just partnered up with Blueberry Bay's first ever talking cat detective. Along with his ragtag gang of human and animal helpers, Octo-Cat is determined to save the day... so long as it doesn't interfere with his schedule.

Start with book 1, *Kitty Confidential*.

MERLIN'S MAGICAL MYSTERIES

Gracie Springs is not a witch... but her cat is. Now she must help to keep his secret or risk spending the rest of her life in some magical prison. Too bad trouble seems to find them at every turn!

Start with book 1, *Merlin Takes a Familiar*.

PARANORMAL TEMP AGENCY

Tawny Bigford's simple life takes a turn for the magical when she stumbles upon her landlady's murder and is recruited by a talking black cat named Fluffikins to take over the deceased's role as the official Town Witch for Beech Grove, Georgia.

Start with book 1, ***Witch for Hire***.

CLAW & ORDER

Moss O'Malley isn't a real cat, and he's not a real cop either. Yet here here he is, serving and protecting while stuck in this suit of fur. That's what happens when you're a shifter con man who's been caught in the act. He's no narc, but he'll also do whatever it takes to stay out of that horrible cat rescue-slash-prison.

Start with book 1, ***Paws & Probable Cause***.

THE MYSTERIES OF MOONLIGHT MANOR (WITH TRIXIE SILVERTALE)

Sydney Coleman has it all—until she doesn't. No sooner does she launch her bed and breakfast, than a trio of ghosts turn up oppose her at every turn. They insist she solve the murder of their mistress, but Sydney is desperate for cash. If she can't book some guests fast, her haunted mansion is utterly doomed.

Start with book 1, ***Moonlight & Mischief***.

THE MEOWING MEDIUM (WITH L.A. BORUFF)

Mags McAllister lives a simple life making candles for tourists in historic Larkhaven, Georgia. But when a cat with mismatched eyes enters her life, she finds herself with the ability to see into the realm of spirits... Now the ghosts of people long dead have started coming to her for help solving their cold cases.

Start with book 1, *Secrets of the Specter*.

CONNECT WITH MOLLY

Sign up for my newsletter and get a special digital prize pack for joining, including an exclusive story, *Meowy Christmas Mayhem*, fun quiz, and lots of cat pictures!

mollymysteries.com/subscribe

Have you ever wanted to talk to animals? You can chat with Octo-Cat and help him solve an exclusive online mystery here:

mollymysteries.com/chat

JOIN MOLLY'S READER CLUB

If you ever wished you could converse with cats, here's your opportunity! This is me officially inviting you into my whacky inner world as part of my Cozy Kitty Club.

For those who just can't get enough of my zany cat characters and their hapless humans, this club will provide weekly (sometimes daily) new content to devour.

From early access to exclusive stories, behind-the-scenes trivia to never-before-released bonus content, and even some signed books and swag thrown in for fun, the CKC has a lot to love.

Come check it out at:
www.MollyMysteries.com/club

Made in the USA
Las Vegas, NV
13 September 2023

77461619R00150